Elena had never been kissed by a man before.

Yet she knew, as Auhan's lips left hers, she would never want to kiss another. She had been falling in love with Auhan for the last several days. Now, with his kiss, she was certain. She had stopped "falling" and was wholly, totally "in" love.

"Dear Elena." He caressed the side of her mouth with his fingertip.

"Dear Auhan," she returned. With a sigh as soft as the breeze, she rubbed her cheek against his hand.

After a moment, the most enchanting moment of both their lives, he whispered into her ear, "Dear Elena, where do we go from here?"

She knew what he was asking.

But she also knew she did not want to answer him.

Her answer would be the same as his.

And it was one neither wanted to voice.

Until he made a decision about Christ and resolved his problems, they couldn't take their relationship any further. A wide chasm of theological thoughts and beliefs separated them.

But he was waiting for an answer. She opened her eyes and twisted her head toward the bow of the ship. "How about—New York?"

TAYLOR JAMES is married to a physician and the mother of two, nearly grown children. A native of Virginia, she loves traveling the world over, seeing new places, and meeting new people. She combines her traveling experiences with her love of writing, history, and God to write stories which are both uplifting and informative.

Her favorite Bible verses are to be found in Paul's letter to the Philippians: "Therefore God exalted him to the highest place and gave him the name that is above every name, that at the name of Jesus every knee should bow, in heaven and on earth and under the earth, and every tongue confess that Jesus Christ is Lord, to the glory of God the Father" (2:9–11 NIV). This truth is what she hopes to convey in all her novels.

Remnant of Light

Taylor James

Heartsong Presents

In memory of the twentieth-century martyrs around the world, who number more than those who died for their faith in all other centuries combined. . .

And for Peter Terbush. A fine son, brother, man, friend. . . hero. He gave his life that another might live.

A note from the author:
I love to hear from my readers! You may correspond with me by writing: **Taylor James
Author Relations
PO Box 719
Uhrichsville, OH 44683**

ISBN 1-58660-315-9

REMNANT OF LIGHT

All Scripture quotations, unless otherwise noted, are taken from the King James Version of the Bible.

All of the characters and events in this book are fictitious. Any resemblance to actual persons, living or dead, or to actual events is purely coincidental.

Cover illustration by Victoria Lisi and Julius.

PRINTED IN THE U.S.A.

prologue

"And unto the angel of the church in Smyrna write; These things saith the first and the last, which was dead, and is alive; I know thy works, and tribulation, and poverty, (but thou art rich) and I know the blasphemy of them which say they are Jews, and are not, but are the synagogue of Satan. Fear none of those things which thou shalt suffer: behold, the devil shall cast some of you into prison, that ye may be tried; and ye shall have tribulation ten days: be thou faithful unto death, and I will give thee a crown of life. He that hath an ear, let him hear what the Spirit saith unto the churches; He that overcometh shall not be hurt of the second death."
Revelation 2:8–11

By late afternoon in the ancient Christian city of Smyrna, enemy troops were lighting twenty fires for each one extinguished by the fire brigade. The smell of the burning city infiltrated the very fabric of the populace as only smoke can. With the billowing smoke came all the fear that uncontrollable fire brings.

Elena Apostologlou and her sister, Sophia, had sewn treasures—money, jewels, and important papers—into each of their garments in the hope something might survive their trek to the safety of the Theatre de Smyrna, an American enclave in the city. Whispering a prayer, Elena followed her sister and their beloved father, Andreas, from the sanctuary of their villa.

As soon as they stepped through the massive front door of their neoclassical home and into the quayside road, the trio experienced the full measure of their city's ransacking. Over the five-day span since the Turkish army had occupied the city again, the sounds of looting and killing had seeped through the thick walls of their home. Yet nothing compared to being out and among the carnage.

The scene looked like something out of the Middle Ages. Elena's senses filled with fiendish displays of barbaric butchery, and she instinctively drew closer to her family. They exchanged frightened looks of disbelief as they witnessed the almost diabolical delight the soldiers found in causing others agony. Like a sweat-drenching nightmare, the late afternoon sky glowed orange and red, while clouds of smoke, ash, and embers descended upon them all.

But the sounds were even worse than the abominable sights. The frantic cries of humans and animals permeated the heavy air and filled Elena's head with a vile timbre. She could focus on an individual cry of pain, yet still hear the wail of a mass agony of souls. The anguished din rose commensurate to the roar of the fire now breathing down on their city like a vast, evil, flame-throwing dragon.

The thick crowd of people moved as one body toward the choppy, churning water of Smyrna's famous sea harbor, where they would hopefully find a launch that would take them to a ship. The pain of seeing his beloved city in the clutches of this antichrist had already taxed her father's weak heart to its limit. So Elena followed Sophia in a deliberately slow pace.

She could feel as well as hear walls crashing in the fire several streets up, and the ground shook beneath them, a man-made earthquake. They were within sight of their father's office building when the thundering hooves of a Turkish cavalry filled the road. A report of rifle fire re-sounded through the crowd.

Pandemonium reigned.

The three of them could do nothing more than crouch and duck their heads down low. There was nowhere for them to go. People screamed all around them. Camels, chickens, dogs, horses raced around, trampling and being trampled in their frightened frenzy. And still the shots rang out; indiscriminate ones meant to terrify and kill. They accomplished both in a horrible way.

With an arm around both his daughters' shoulders, Elena's father held them under his protective grip and struggled to keep his children safe. She could hear him reciting the Lord's Prayer.

Elena kept waiting to feel the cold bite of metal rip through her skin. She watched the man in front of them throw his little girl, then his wife, upon the ground. He had no sooner flung his own body over the both of them than a shot hit him and made his body stiffen, then relax. When Elena reached out to try and help, the shot she had been dreading hit its mark.

But the bullet didn't hit her.

It plowed into the dear flesh of her father's body, which had been protecting her own, and the force slammed him against her.

"Baba!" Elena and Sophia screamed together as he crumpled to the ground.

"Baba, no!" Elena dropped to the earth beside him. Where the bullet had pierced him, his life flowed in a steady stream of dark red. She pressed her hand, sheathed in a white linen glove, against the wound. But despite her best efforts, his blood—his life—continued to seep out. Turning her glove crimson, it ran into the pavement of the city that had been

home to their ancestors for three thousand years.

"*Baba!*" She shook her head in horror at the sight of the red liquid now trickling from the side of his mouth as well. "No," she rasped. "No. This war cannot have you! Please. No!"

"Elena." Sophia spoke sharply from the other side of their father, and Elena looked into her tear-filled eyes. "Listen," she commanded. "He is trying to tell us something."

In their home of safe haven over the past few days, she had witnessed the deaths of so many refugees from this Greco-Turkish War that she now recognized all the signs. Their father, like the others, would soon leave them. With tears of despair washing unchecked down her face, Elena leaned in to hear her father's last words. As she did, she faded into another reality amid the volley of bullets whistling around them and the resulting mayhem.

"My daughters," he choked through the blood that filled his mouth. "Fear none of those things which thou shalt suffer." He admonished them with the same love that they had never doubted. Elena immediately recognized his words as those spoken by the Lord to the church in their very own city.

"God's truth, His wisdom, and His light will guide you." His gaze lit upon Sophia, his eldest child, then turned to his younger one. Elena bit her lower lip as she nodded her understanding of his choice of words. Her deceased, American mother's name, Letta, meant "truth," Sophia's, "wisdom," and her own "light," all attributes of the Lord's and of those who follow in His footsteps.

Blood dripped from her father's mouth, and he coughed weakly. Elena felt certain that his heart was giving out, yet he struggled for enough breath to speak his final words to them before he left.

"Promise me. . .you will escape this tribulation," he managed to say as he fought for air. ". . .And you. . .will both live. . .to be. . .very happy, very kind. . .old ladies. . ." His lips turned up into a weak smile. ". . .Older than I am now," he rasped.

"*Baba*. . ." Elena bit her lower lip and shook her head back and forth. "Don't—"

"Please. . . ," he begged, and from the gurgling sound coming out with his words Elena knew that his lungs were fast filling with blood and drowning him. She had never felt more helpless. "I know. . .you never. . .break your. . ." He stopped speaking, but Elena knew that it wasn't because of want.

Seeing and understanding the need in his eyes, both girls vigorously nodded their heads. "We promise, *Baba*. . . ," they spoke together, assuring their dear father of their pledge.

"We will grow old. . . ," Sophia declared.

"Very old," Elena agreed.

"And. . .bitter. . .ness. . . ?" He slightly shook his head. "No. . . ."

"No. No bitterness, *Baba*," Elena quickly assured him. His entire life he had preached against hatred, anger, and bitterness. She wouldn't dishonor him now by letting it grow. "No bitterness against those who did this to you."

His lips curved up slightly at their corners, and he gave them one last smile. His eyes then turned to something beyond their shoulders, and his face, in spite of his pain, radiated an otherworldly light as he whispered out a perfect sentence, his last. "He has come to guide me home."

"*Baba*. . ." As Elena called out, his face paled before her gaze, and his lips, beneath the red of the blood still trickling out between them, slowly turned to blue. She pushed her hand harder against the hole the lead had carved into his beloved flesh, a child's futile effort to keep a much-loved parent with her, if only for a few seconds longer.

"No. . . ," she whined. "No. . .come with us, *Baba*."

She leaned harder still on the wound. "Don't turn us into orphans," she implored of his gentle blue eyes, eyes that now gazed unseeingly up at her, making the lids of her own squeeze shut in agony. "Don't leave us," she cried, sounding more like the little girl of five she had been when her mother had died than a young woman of eighteen.

Even when she felt her sister's fingers wrap around her own and remove her hand from her father's wound, she couldn't move. "Elena, look at him," Sophia commanded, a measure of the sublime touching her tone. "He is not here any longer. Our dear *Baba*. . .this body is no longer his home. Look. He has left it. He has moved on to a better place."

Through her excruciating, breath-robbing pain, Elena could, by a miracle of God, hear the wisdom in her sister's voice. Like a resounding thunder, and yet, as soft as a caress, her tone was not something she could ignore. There was truth in her sister's words, a truth that demanded attention. Slowly opening her eyes, Elena looked, and as she did, she saw the evidence of Sophia's testimony. The man who had been their father was no longer there. He looked as if he had come out of the body that had been his home for seventy-two years and moved—somewhere else.

"For God so loved the world, that he gave his only begotten Son, that whosoever believeth in him should not perish, but have everlasting life." Elena heard Sophia speak the most loving, the most truthful words of the Lord's, found in the Gospel of John: John, the very apostle of Christ who had taught Polycarp, the first bishop of Smyrna.

"It's true," Elena whispered with a joy only a Christian could feel, could comprehend, in the face of death. "Our father has only departed. He has not perished." The radiance she felt belied the horror of what she had just experienced.

Sophia nodded her head, and, while not taking her eyes

from the beloved face, she reached into her pocket and pulled out a handkerchief of the purest white. Gently, she wiped the blood from her father's gray mustache, his beard. That done, she looked at Elena, and, wordlessly, they discarded their blood-soaked gloves, and together they reached out and closed their father's unseeing eyes.

A bullet whizzed past their heads, bringing into focus once again the bedlam that surrounded them. As Elena looked around, she saw the man and the woman who had been running ahead of them. She had seen the man die. But as she looked through the eerie light cast by the roaring, citywide fire, she now saw that his wife had been killed too. With a groan that sounded like something issuing from a wounded animal, she lunged toward the couple.

Sophia grabbed her arm and held her back. "Elena. What are you doing? Have you gone mad?"

"The girl!" Elena shouted. "They threw themselves on top of their little girl to protect her. Even if she survived the barrage of bullets, she won't survive much longer without air."

Understanding and horror dawned simultaneously in Sophia's face. Sophia joined her in pushing aside the large man and his wife. Too numb in the nightmare of the moment, Elena felt nothing for the couple. But they had died protecting their child, and she knew that they must get the girl out from under her parents' combined dead weight.

Blood covered the little girl, and, for a moment, Elena feared that the child too had fallen victim to a Turkish bullet. But when air reached her small face and she opened her eyes, Elena knew the girl was uninjured. At least physically.

"Come, Darling." She held out her arms to the girl. The young girl was in a trance, but upon seeing Elena, she blinked.

"Elena?"

She looked closely at the features of the little girl, now

camouflaged beneath the blood and the dirt covering her face.

"Rose! Is that you?" Elena exclaimed as she recognized her favorite charge from the previous July. Of Armenian ancestry, eight-year-old Rose had been one of Elena's swimming students. She was one of the sweetest little girls in the world. Her kindness toward others was well known within the American school she attended in Smyrna, both among the teachers and students.

"Elena!" The girl wrapped her arms around Elena's neck, but as she did, her gaze fell upon her parents lying to the side. Backing up from Elena, she caught sight of the blood on her arms, on her chest, on her legs, and just about everywhere on her body. Her screams rent the air.

"*Mairig! Hairig! Mairig! Hairig!*" Over and over in her native Armenian she cried out for her parents. A litany of despair. Of pain. Of mourning.

Afraid that Rose would attract the attention of the soldiers, who would, without remorse, run her through with a sword, Elena pulled her close in a tight hug, quieting her mouth against her chest. "You mustn't cry out." She nodded over to the soldiers who were still firing into the crowds but had moved down a bit farther. "They will come back and hurt us. And your mother and father don't want that. They gave their lives so that you might live. And live you will."

"But how? . . . I'm so. . .afraid," Rose whimpered, and her grief-stricken face, smeared with her parents' blood, touched deeply into Elena's soul. "Without my *Mairig* and *Hairig*. . . ," she squeaked out, but bravely gulped back her cries. Even though tears still streamed down her little face, she didn't scream out again.

"You have Sophia and me. And now we have you. From this moment on, you are our sister." She glanced over at Sophia for confirmation of the idea. As Sophia nodded her golden head in affirmation, Elena continued, "We were all three made orphans this night, little Rose. But we will be safe."

"How do you know?" The little girl's soft wails rose to a piercing crescendo. But she bit her lips to keep from screaming, and blood, this time her own precious supply, seeped out from between her teeth. Elena knew Rose had plenty of experience at stifling screams. In all likelihood, she and her parents had been hiding from the Turkish soldiers in the suffocating heat of their home's attic since the soldiers had entered the city five days earlier. But, like Elena's family, Rose and her parents had been forced from their home when the fires were set.

"Because my trust is not placed in just a person," Elena answered the little girl. "Nor in those ships out there." She motioned to the ships—American, British, French, Italian, and more, all ostensibly allies of Greece—which the Christians of the city had thought of as safe haven. "Only with God. He will keep us safe. He has to, so that my sister, Sophia, and I can fulfill our *secret* promise to our father." She nodded toward her sister as she spoke, purposefully placing emphasis on the word secret.

Rose's dark eyes widened. "What *secret* promise?"

"To live a long life."

"They are coming back this way!" Sophia shouted out in terror. "We must go!"

Elena glanced up to see only daggers, dripping with blood, marching in their direction. Grabbing Rose in her arms, she turned to look one last time at the precious body that had housed her father. Sending it a final, sad smile and a blown kiss, she turned, and, with Sophia by her side, they ran as fast as their feet could carry them away from the approaching soldiers.

"We have to get to the Theatre de Smyrna," she heard Sophia shout from her side.

"I know." But a frantic glance in its direction showed that the way to the theater they had been instructed to take by the American consul general was now cut off by Turkish soldiers. Their only chance was to run the next street up. "Maybe the consul general hasn't left the consulate yet," Elena said. Panting and sweating in the heat of the city burning on a hot summer day, they took off up a side road in that direction. Elena still clutched Rose in her arms.

Just as they reached the point where they could see the stately neoclassical edifice of the American consulate, they caught sight of the consul general and his wife rushing down a guarded pathway and past the American sailors on their way to their car. Even under the best of circumstances, Elena, a very good athlete, knew that she wouldn't be able to reach him or the American servicemen in time. A sea of frightened people blocked their way.

As still as a statue, except for the tears that ran unchecked down her cheeks, Elena watched the car move through the crowd in the opposite direction from where they stood.

"He's gone. The consul general is gone," Sophia breathed out.

"May God protect him," Elena whispered into Rose's blood-matted hair. "Next to our father, the consul general is one of the best men I have ever met."

Sophia nodded. "Just like the Greek soldier, Christos, who brought the wounded one to our house last Thursday."

Elena knew the soldier had made a great impression on her sister. A huge man, Christos had carried his friend for days across battlefields to what he had thought would be the safety of Smyrna before going to join his routed army at their debarkation point. Now he represented to them all the individuals who were trying to help people survive in this city of anarchy.

Even beyond that, Elena was aware that something wonderful, perhaps something God-inspired, had passed between her sister and the big man. And she sensed the importance of Sophia's thoughts about him—in this world turned upside down and inside out.

Until the previous Saturday, Smyrna had been considered one of the most beautiful cities in the world. Some even said it was second only to Paris. Now both its beauty and its identity were being obliterated forever. Elena knew Sophia was nearly in shock over the many losses they had faced in such a short time. "Yes, Sophia, just like Christos."

She grunted when a large woman bumped against her shoulder. The road was filled to capacity with frantic people running for safety.

"All of our friends will assume that we're safely at the Theatre de Smyrna," Sophia stated in a monotone when the car with the consul general could no longer be seen. Her entire demeanor spoke of a defeated person. "We. . .are. . . alone."

Elena sharpened her gaze on her sister. Through the smoke-filled air around them, she could see Sophia's trembling lips. Fear gripped her as she heard the despondency creeping into Sophia's voice.

"No, Sophia," she admonished. "We are *not* alone. God is with us. He will see us safely out of Smyrna. Don't get discouraged. Please," Elena begged. "Don't despair. I need you."

Sophia had been named perfectly. Wisdom filled the very essence of her nature, and Elena could tell as her sister breathed in and out deeply, trying to find enough oxygen in the smoky atmosphere to feed her system, that she was endeavoring to keep the debilitating, negative emotion from gripping hold of her. After a long moment, she reached out for Elena's hand and squeezed it. "As I need you, Dear."

Rose wiggled to be put down and placed her small hand over those of the two older girls. "And I need both of you," she said.

Elena offered the young girl a smile of comfort. "We are family now. Sisters. For always." As she said the words, she looked down. A gasp escaped her lips when she glimpsed their interlocked hands.

All three of them bore the sacrificial blood of their parents.

Elena knew she would remember the sight throughout the remainder of her days. But for now, the sight made her all the more determined to find a way out of their burning city. Their parents died trying to get them to safety. Elena refused to let their deaths be in vain.

one

And now for a little space grace hath been shewed from
the LORD our God, to leave us a remnant to escape.
Ezra 9:8

Elena awoke to sunlight on her face. And with the light came a good heat. A normal heat. A heat that didn't claw at her lungs or burn her skin.

Yet even with the realization, another pain, a deep pain, started somewhere around her stomach and rose with bile to her throat. A heart-rending knowledge filled her thoughts. This would be the first day of her life that she would not see her father or wish him a good morning. An unbidden, keening moan came from the depths of her soul as she cried for the father she had loved.

Elena knew that her father was now forever safe. She knew he was alive in Christ. She accepted, with childlike faith, the fact that he was in heaven experiencing a grand reunion with her mother.

But, oh, she missed him. She missed him so badly. And a vision rose within her—a tormenting vision of her father's body lying on that dirty street with the blood flowing out of his mouth from the mortal wound. Her heart filled with a pain that seemed to flow through her veins and pumped through every vessel in her body, even to the tiniest capillary.

She realized the hurt of having been orphaned at the age of

eighteen, in such a terrible way, would cripple her if she allowed it to take control. She couldn't let it rule her.

She forced herself to stop the sounds of mourning that flowed from her innermost being, and she opened her eyes. They were caked with salt from her tears and from the sea she had swum in the previous night in escaping Smyrna. She had to rub her fingers over them to help pry the lids apart. Gritty and rough, the salt pulled at them, pulled many of her lashes out too, but she hardly noticed.

She looked up to the sky. It wasn't the Aegean blue she was used to seeing. Rather, it was vividly red. The sun seemed to have a hard time filtering its rays through the smoke of Smyrna's smoldering remains.

Seagulls flew in the strong wind above the Italian flag, which rose above the stern of the ship. Elena's gaze stayed glued to the squawking gulls. They sang their same, ancient song.

Elena's chapped and cracked lips turned up slightly at their corners, and she smiled, even though the taste of blood accompanied the movement. Gulls were something normal in a world turned traitor to her, something to feast her eyes upon, to draw comfort from, to focus upon now, and to live.

She watched them play in the sky for a few minutes, then slowly turned her head to look for Sophia and Rose and the others who had shared the little rowboat with them in escaping Smyrna. She smiled when she saw Rose's heart-shaped face as she lay next to her, safe and secure. Sophia slept on the other side of the child, and the other women and children occupied the deck just beyond her.

She squinted. She didn't see Christos, Sophia's Greek soldier, who had miraculously appeared the previous night in their time of greatest need.

They had returned to their home for the rowboat, which Elena had remembered their father storing in the garden shed. There, Christos had not only saved them from rape and death at the hands of a gang of Turkish soldiers, but he had helped them escape the burning city as well. Elena knew, even with the precious rowboat, they would never have accomplished their flight without Christos's strength.

Not seeing any men at all, she assumed that Christos was sleeping in a section cordoned off specifically for them. She turned the other way, and her eyes widened when she saw she was lying along the edge of the ship with only an inch separating her from a fall into the choppy sea. She was desperately thirsty but even more exhausted. A kind person had covered her during the night, and now she pulled the blanket tighter around her shoulders and scooted closer to Rose. Realizing that her head was resting upon a ringed lifesaver, she only had the energy to wrap her arm through it before oblivion, sweet and deep, overtook her once again and she slept.

But it wasn't the sweet sleep of an untroubled soul.

The ship swayed back and forth in the wind, first rising high out of the water only to slam back down into the sea. The push of humanity, as on the burning streets of Smyrna, seemed to have followed Elena. She felt herself being shoved against something both sharp and long. She struggled to awaken, even as her fingers clawed at the pillow her head rested upon, but she couldn't pull herself into consciousness—not even when she felt herself falling. Falling. Falling.

Only when her body submerged into the sea and the water sucked her into its depth did her eyes open. Only then did she know that her nightmare was once again a reality, and she had been swept off the boat into the deep blue sea.

When she had fallen overboard, her body was still wrapped in the thick blanket, and it was now pulling her down into the water's depths. She struggled to free herself from the blanket's weight. Thankfully, she had discarded her shoes last night when she and Christos opted to swim next to the rowboat in order to allow more room for women and children in the boat's hull. She would have failed in her attempts to survive now with the added weight of shoes. With her lungs nearly bursting, she pushed the heavy blanket from her. She followed the rising bubbles of oxygen and pushed herself toward the surface light using all her strength.

Waves crashed upon her face.

She gulped in seawater, which irritated her already raw throat. Gasping and coughing, she struggled to keep afloat. If her hands hadn't grazed against the lifesaver she had rested her head upon during the night, she doubted that she would have been able to get her breathing under control as well as keep herself afloat.

Clutching the ring, she turned her back to the waves and coughed out the water that threatened to fill her lungs. Moments later, she looked toward the ship. It was steaming away from her, the black smoke coming out of its smokestack like a flag of mourning, mocking her.

No one—not Sophia or Rose, or even Christos—seemed to realize that she had fallen overboard. As the ship moved farther and farther away, Elena knew that she was on her own. By the time those on board realized that she was missing, they would be long gone. And she would appear as nothing more than a dot on the sea.

A sense of surrealism assailed Elena. *Had she really fallen off the ship*? Was it possible for her to have lived through the horror of seeing her father and hundreds of other Christians killed, to have witnessed the utter destruction of Smyrna, only to tumble from their rescue vessel to be drowned at sea?

She felt so utterly miserable; she knew it was all too true. Her throat burned. Her back ached from her fall against the hard sea surface. The salt water stung the numerous raw blisters on her face and hands caused by flying embers as they fled the city.

A tidal wave of panic swelled from the pit of her stomach and swept over her. But Elena knew she couldn't allow it. She knew enough about people washed overboard to understand that panic was more her enemy right now than the never-ending sea that surrounded her.

If she didn't panic, she would survive.

She made her body breathe in and out, calmly, smoothly, while she forced her mind to consider her advantages. The rough seas were beginning to calm, and she could swim. She had a life ring, and she was in the Aegean Sea, a body of water that was filled with boats and islands. A new day was dawning, so she had at least twelve hours before darkness engulfed her. And the water this time of year was not dangerously cold. She knew that Sophia, Rose, and Christos were safe. But, most of all, she knew that she wasn't really alone.

God was with her. He was her trust. He would give her all she needed to survive. And even though she couldn't begin to imagine what good He could bring out of her falling into the sea, especially after all that had happened during the last five days, she would trust Him to provide for her. Now was definitely not the time to stop trusting.

As the sun rose higher into the sky, Elena settled into the life ring, pulled her body as close as she could to conserve her body heat, and she waited.

She was so tired. And so very thirsty. "I thirst." The Lord's words as He hung upon the cross, held new meaning for her.

After floating in the sea for a couple of hours, her body was freezing, and she had to kick her feet to generate warmth. However, her head was burning in the rays of the sun. She could see her cheeks expanding below her eyes and knew that her face was swelling severely. The burns she had sustained in the fire had been minor, but after baking all day in the sun and soaking in saltwater, she shuddered to think how they would become.

Wiggling around, careful not to lose her grip on the life preserver, Elena reached down to remove her petticoat in order to use it as a covering for her head. As she did, her hands brushed against something hard and round in the pocket of her dress. She frowned, wondering if some sort of fish had taken up residency in her pocket.

But remembrance swooped in on her when her numb hands inspected what was caught in the billowing folds of her dress. A grin, which made her cracked lips bleed again, split across her swollen face.

An apple!

She remembered she had pushed the fruit into her dress pocket just before leaving home the day before. "Oh, dear Lord," she croaked. If she had had enough liquid in her system for tears, they would have fallen down her cheeks in blessed relief. For Elena knew that this apple might just save her life.

Of all her father's wealth, this apple, which their cook had bought the previous, peaceful week at the fruit market, was, at this moment, the most precious thing he had owned. It was worth more than all the gold, all the works of art, all the money he had had in banks, because this apple, God's very bounty, would sustain Andreas Apostologlou's youngest daughter's life.

Elena bit into the fruit, and the sound—that wonderful popping sound—reverberated in her head. For that half-hour in which Elena kept company with her apple, she didn't even feel the crinkles of her shriveling skin. She forgot where she was, how thirsty, how tired, how cold her body felt, and how hot her head burned. The apple became more than just nourishment and liquid to her. It became Elena's hold on life.

When she had eaten three-fourths of the fruit, she forced herself to stop. Nothing could be seen on the horizon, and she knew that she would have to keep the rest for later. If she were indeed called upon to spend the night in the sea, she would need the apple to get through it. Just to hold it, lick it would help. That decided, she placed it back into her pocket for safekeeping.

And she waited.

And as she waited, she prayed.

If God couldn't send a boat to her, she prayed He would at least send her some sort of company. A seagull, or a turtle, even a school of friendly fish. She knew God was with her, but still, she felt so lonely—something she had never been before. There had always been someone with her. Most often her father or Sophia. But now, she had lost both, and even her new little sister, Rose. All within a matter of hours.

"Lord, Lord," she implored, calling out to Him as she had so many times during her eighteen years. "Please send a boat. . .someone. . .don't let me stay out here all night alone. I can't. . .can't. . ." She groaned from deep within her soul.

She had no sooner stopped praying than she saw something moving toward her. She blinked her eyes.

But it wasn't a boat. It seemed to be swimming in the water. A dolphin?

She slightly shook her burning head. No. The form wasn't slicing through the sea like those streamlined mammals normally did.

A dog then? But it couldn't be.

She squinted her eyes and tried to focus on the object. It sure looked like a dog. Yet the idea that a dog could survive out in the Aegean Sea was absurd.

She squeezed her eyes shut and shook her head before opening them once more. Perhaps she was hallucinating.

Chills had been racking her body, and she hadn't been able to stop coughing for the last couple of hours. She was quite certain that she was running a high fever.

But as the object came closer, she also knew that she wasn't imagining things.

It *was* a dog.

As big, brown eyes gazed up at her from a sopping face, the fluke of a dolphin's tail emerged from behind the dog, and Elena knew how the dog was being kept above water. The dog used his weak paws to paddle up beside her, and Elena made a sound that was as much a laugh as she could manage.

"Oh my, oh my," she said as she reached for his forelegs. Growing up along the shore of the Aegean, she had heard all the legends about dolphins and how they saved shipwrecked people. But never had Elena considered them to be more than just sailor's fancy, and even less, something that might happen in modern days. Elena knew all she had heard was true when the grinning face of a large dolphin swam from beneath the dog and greeted her with a high-pitched squeal. It seemed to be giving her an admonishment to care for the canine creature. Then and there, she was firmly convinced that dolphins really *do* understand, and they *do* help those in need.

Pulling the dog close to her, Elena somehow managed to drape his legs across the life preserver without upsetting her own hold. "Here, Boy, here," she cooed to him. Elena knew if she could see his tail, it would be wagging slowly from side to side. As it was, he looked at her with grateful eyes and flicked his dry tongue about her face. The dolphin swam around them like a sentinel guarding treasure.

Even though Elena understood that her prayer for company

had been answered, she also recognized that the dog, unquestionably another refugee from the destruction of Smyrna, was in a desperate condition. He needed what remained of her apple more than she did. Without the liquid it would afford him, she was sure he would die. And without him, Elena was almost certain she would too.

Reaching into her pocket, she pulled out the apple, and slowly, with love, she fed him. With each bite the dog's eyes seemed to light up a bit more. After he had finished, she laid her head against his and his breath—life—fanned her face. With the dolphin swimming around them both, she rested.

However, after awhile, her chills and cough threatened to make Elena totally lose her hold on reality. Just then, the dolphin nudged her softly. Elena watched as it spun around and started slicing though the water away from them.

"No. . .Don't go. . . ," she croaked out, fear lacing her voice. "Please don't go. . ." But it turned back to her only long enough to whistle something in his language before taking off at a high-speed swim toward the sun, which sat just above the surface of the sea like a bobbing ball.

Wrapping her arms tighter around the dog, Elena couldn't help the dry sobs that she poured out onto his neck. Where the dog was companionship of an earthbound nature, the dolphin had been not just company but a source of security as well. She was in his watery world, his domain, and somehow having him close had made her feel protected.

But now he was gone, and she was so cold, so tired, so miserable, that her body didn't even feel like her own.

Still, she had the dog. She had to focus on this blessing. And he needed her as much as she needed him. With the sea lapping all around them, they clung together, eye to eye, his ragged breath mingling with her own. And they were the best of friends.

Even though all seemed hopeless, even though she had cried as if it was, Elena knew that all hope was not lost. She had to live, so she *would* live. Her father's dying request had been for Sophia and her to live to be very old ladies. Elena, for her part, wouldn't disappoint him. Besides, she had to survive in order to meet Sophia and Rose at the Lincoln Memorial in Washington the following May.

She thanked God for their having made that impromptu date the previous May when they—her father, Sophia, and she—had attended the dedication ceremony of the memorial built to honor Abraham Lincoln. A shudder shook her body as she considered how she would have located her sisters otherwise. She had no fear that Sophia would forget their planned picnic on May 30, 1923—a year to the day after that moving ceremony. She was certain that they would be reunited there. Because of this assurance, at least Elena knew that she didn't have to worry about never finding her loved ones again.

Time passed.

Elena wasn't sure how much.

Through fits of coughing, she watched the sun sink into the sea. With its disappearance, she closed her eyes. She didn't want to see the night. To feel it was enough.

An hour passed—maybe a little less, maybe a little more— while she and the dog she had named "Buddy" hugged one another. Suddenly, she felt a change in her canine friend. His ears twitched. And then his head moved against her cheek. When a small yap came out of him, Elena's eyes popped open.

And she gasped.

The silhouette of a ship loomed on the horizon against the backdrop of a majestic sky. And the ship was gliding across the sea toward them.

Elena's befuddled brain knew that she had to get its attention somehow, otherwise it would plow straight past them. Just as she started to slap her numb and impotent hands against the water, at least fifty streamlined bodies jumped up and out of the sea and started dancing and singing around the two castaways. Elena's mouth dropped open in amazement as she surmised that her dolphin friend had returned with his pod and that they were performing a dance—a rescue dance for her and the dog—upon the moonlit surface of the Aegean Sea.

The dog gave a little bark to the dolphin as it swam up next to them and gently nudged both of them with his pointy nose. Elena reached out and rubbed him. "Thank you," she croaked. The dolphin's smile seemed to broaden. With a happy glint in his eyes, he squeaked in his dolphin way, then swam off to frolic with the members of his pod.

Through eyes that were practically swollen shut from saltwater blisters and burns, Elena watched their ballet, and, thankfully, those on board the ship did too. Just as a light shone down upon the company of playful dolphins, and thus upon her and the dog, unconsciousness claimed Elena. As on the previous night when their little rowboat had been rescued by the Italian ship in Smyrna's harbor, she slipped into the sweet, sweet release of knowing others would now care for her.

While she slept, the moonlight dance of dolphins and the sweet breath of a dog stayed within her mind and calmed her soul.

two

Jesus answered and said unto him, Verily, verily,
I say unto thee, Except a man be born again,
he cannot see the kingdom of God.
John 3:3

"I'm fearful that she may have pneumonia."

A woman's pleasant but concerned voice sounded as though she stood far above her. Yet even as Elena endeavored to identify the speaker, blackness claimed her once again.

"*Baba*, no! *Baba!*" Elena startled to a hazy wakefulness to hear someone screaming. "Sophia, Rose, Christos, come back! Mamma!"

At the final word, the realization hit her. She was the crying girl.

"Shhh, Darling, shhh," Again, she heard the sweet voice speak to her. Could it be her mother? Elena's befuddled brain wondered. Had she gone to be with her mother in heaven? But, no. Heaven had no pain, no confusion. And Elena's body was filled with both.

A cooling cloth pressed against her forehead. "Be still, dear girl. Be still. You are safe." Elena grabbed hold of the admonishment like she had so recently grabbed hold of the life preserver. She forced herself to quiet down, and soon oblivion claimed her, something much sweeter than the chilled and aching reality of a body that had betrayed her. Consciousness hurt—hurt more than Elena, who had never been sick a day in her life, wanted to hurt. She slept, but

28

whenever she detected the cooling hands of someone lifting her head and pouring liquid down her parched and burning throat, she accepted the offering with a grateful heart.

Although her body slept, her mind didn't. It shifted and shimmered with images.

Images—red and orange—of fire and screams, which could only be doused by replacing them with the sweetness of a dog's breath against her cheek or the dance of dolphins on a starry night.

And a ship.

The mental picture of a ship before her in the sea would bring relief from the raging of the fire, the screams of people running, running, always running.

And she would sleep.

Until the next time.

But somehow even with the terrible nightmares filling her fevered sleep, Elena knew that they were exactly that.

Nightmares.

No longer reality.

And even though they startled her, they were not to be compared to the living ones she had so recently experienced. In the realm of bad dreams, there came the cooling hands of a mother to soothe her. In the actual days of wartime reality, the real-life nightmare world, there had been no comforting touch.

Time passed. But Elena had no idea how to count out the days or hours. Only the woman with the calming hands knew, the wonderful hands Elena would forever trust, forever remember. They were "mother" hands, hands Elena had missed for the last thirteen years of her life. Hands for which Elena expectantly waited to see the face to whom they belonged.

☙

"*Anne*," Auhan addressed his mother, Fatima, in Turkish as

he reached down to rub the ache he knew had to be in her slender shoulders. "You must rest."

His mother hadn't caught more than an occasional nap in days. She had single-handedly doctored the young woman whom the crew of their little steamship, the *Ionian Star*, had picked out of the Aegean Sea several days earlier. All onboard had affectionately taken to calling the rescued woman, "Dolphin Girl."

His mother squeezed his hand. Then, with a gentle caress, she studied it in the special way that told Auhan she was thinking about her older son, Mehmet. Auhan and his older brother had identical hands, even down to their matching moles just above the knuckle of their right thumbs. He knew his mother wondered where his brother with the same hands might be. Even though many soldiers—both Turkish and Greek—had died in the Greco-Turkish War, Auhan knew that she believed that her eldest child wasn't among the dead. Auhan didn't share his mother's opinion.

With a sigh, she let go of his hand and turned back to the girl. "I cannot let the sea have her, Auhan. It will *not* end like before," she spoke softly but with determination in her tone.

Auhan knew that his mother's mind had now shifted to that of his older sister. She had drowned when she had been fifteen and he only twelve, his brother sixteen.

In the light of the lone candle that burned on the bedside table, Auhan glanced over at his father, Suleiman, who sat on the far bunk in the cabin. The older man's lips pursed together beneath his bushy mustache, and he gave his head a gentle nod, a nod of understanding. Auhan's father, his brother, and he had all thought that they were going to lose this dear woman to a broken heart at that time too.

Auhan turned back to his mother. "This girl will not die." He said the words with a conviction he could not have explained, yet somehow believed. "You have saved her, *Anne*. You." He put the emphasis on his mother's work. Unlike the murmurs to "God" he had heard coming from his mother, he would not let Allah—God—Whomever—have any of the credit. Neither the Muslim Allah nor the Christian God, if there were any difference, was very high on his list of "likes." Auhan seriously doubted that the Almighty would ever be. It wasn't that Auhan didn't believe in Him. He simply didn't like Him. At least not the Almighty he knew.

"*Anne, your* work has saved her," he repeated, and his eyes went to the dog that slumbered at the girl's feet. The sight still amazed him. *A dog, not only in their cabin, but sleeping—sleeping—on a bed.* Amazing and yet wonderful too.

Auhan had always loved the creatures. But the Muslim religion forbade people to have dogs as pets. They believed angels would not enter a house with a dog, and they even ordered all black dogs put to death. Due to his love of dogs, he had secretly spent extra time with their watchdog at their farm, and he was glad his parents hadn't separated the girl and her dog. In his opinion, after what the two had been through together, such a thing would have been cruel.

"Not only have you saved the girl but the dog too, *Anne*," he pronounced and watched with interest as his mother leaned over and gently ran her hand over the golden fur of the dog's long body.

"Poor thing," she murmured with compassion in her tone. "He suffered so much."

The dog had sustained numerous burns to his neck and back, and they estimated he had been in the salty sea for at least a day. His mother had doctored both girl and beast, just as she had doctored Auhan through his bout with malaria the previous year.

Yet, his mother couldn't cure him of his guilt, his doubt,

his deep-seated anger. Auhan was sure no one could ever help him. And since his parents' revelation, all these emotions had only intensified.

Last year, after all he had seen with his own eyes of what had become of many of the Christians who had been forced into cruel winter deportations by his government, his parents had hoped to encourage him. So they confessed that their bloodline was composed more of apostatized Christians— Greeks, from the earliest days of Christianity—than of the Turks from the medieval steppes of Asia. But the knowledge hadn't helped Auhan. He wasn't sure his being descended from an apostatized people was a better alternative.

Besides, if he had both Turkish and Greek blood running through his veins, who was he? He shook his head. He wouldn't let these thoughts play in his mind right now. They were circular ones, which led nowhere except to more disillusionment, more confusion. But the realization occurred to him—there *was* something he could do to help his mother. He could assist her with this girl who had invaded their cabin.

He frowned. "Invade" was a harsh word and the wrong one. It wasn't the girl's fault she had been found adrift upon the sea. But then, whose fault was it? He almost didn't want to know.

"Tell me what to do, *Anne*," he quickly spoke to quiet his mind. "It's past midnight," he said and pointed to the blackness beyond the porthole. "I will care for her as you sleep."

Fatima's tired gaze flitted toward her son. He could tell his offer had startled her, but not any more than the voicing of it had surprised him.

Since the previous year, he had not only deserted from the Turkish army, but he'd deserted from life in general. Deep, dark depression had caused him to have nothing to do with anyone, hardly even with his father or mother. He hadn't wanted it to be that way. It wasn't something he had decided upon. In fact, Auhan hated his behavior. He felt like a prisoner. He was. A prisoner of his mind.

He knew his mother didn't want to leave the girl in anyone else's care, not even the ship's doctoring seaman. But, for him to show an interest in something—someone—would be too enticing an occurrence for her to pass up.

As he anticipated, his mother stood and relinquished the care of the girl to him.

"Every half an hour, spoon a little bit of soup into her mouth," she instructed, motioning to the table behind the girl, which held a covered bowl of broth. A weary, affectionate smile lifted the corners of her mouth as she regarded the girl. "Bless her heart, unlike most who fight liquid being poured into them when so ill, she normally tries to help."

She motioned to a ceramic bowl filled with water on the trunk beside her. "Keep the cloth cool upon her head." Auhan nodded in understanding. He couldn't help but notice that the cloth she had fixed around the girl's golden head was actually one of his mother's own scarves.

"Be careful not to let the burned areas get wet," his mother continued. She pointed to a big burn on the "Dolphin Girl's" left cheek near her ear and to her hand, swathed in the white cloth Fatima had sterilized the moment she had realized the extent of the burns. "Praise God, her burns have not become infected. But they must be kept dry," she admonished.

"I can do that," Auhan nodded and sat on the trunk his mother had been using. "What if she starts to shake?" On occasion, he had noticed the girl's body wracking with chills.

Fatima motioned to the dog at the end of the bed. He had practically recovered after a couple of days of rest and nourishment. However, except when Auhan took him above deck to relieve himself, he didn't leave the girl's side. "He keeps

her feet warm, which is good, because her chills seem to orig-
inate there. If she does start to shiver, you must cover her with
another blanket and rub her arms and legs, but only until the
chills subside. Afterwards her temperature will rise and then
her legs and arms will have to be bathed with spirits to draw
out the fever. Call me if that occurs," she admonished.

Auhan knew his mother wouldn't want him, a young man,
to perform such a deed for the girl. They weren't certain of
the girl's age, but judging by her stylish clothing and youthful physique, his mother had estimated her to be somewhere
between seventeen and twenty years old.

After casting one more loving look in the young girl's
direction, Auhan's mother walked over to his father, who,
standing, sent a grateful look to him for finding a way to get
the woman to take a much-needed rest.

⁂

As his mother slept, Auhan followed all her instructions.

Keeping his distance helped him to retain a small hold on
normal life. Yet, in spite of his need to remain aloof, he saw
something special in this girl. She tugged at his ability to
care and feel—a part of him he thought mortally wounded the
previous year—the day he had come upon the mass grave.

He would never forget that horrific moment. Seeing the
remains of people—old men, woman, children, *babies*—hundreds of them, had broken the fun-loving, youthful part of
Auhan's soul. Even with the repercussions of the Great War
still touching their lives, up until then he had believed the
world was a pretty nice place. Until that moment, he had
never seriously considered the talk in the army camp about
the rulers of his nation ordering the deportation—a conve-
nient term for execution—of so many Christians, people,
perhaps, like the young girl before him. But coming upon
that fresh mass grave had been all the proof Auhan had

needed. Running into the woods nearby, he lost the contents of his stomach as well as any desire to be part of a nation that deliberately killed babies.

Babies. Auhan loved babies. He loved children in general. He had always dreamed of teaching them music. But music had died in him that day too. He glanced over at the leather case that contained his beloved violin. He doubted he would ever play another note.

Shaking his head, he remembered—as much as his brain would allow—the day he happened upon that grave. He had thrown his gun aside and started to walk. He had walked and walked and walked. For days, weeks, he just kept walking. Amazingly, the malaria, which he contracted somewhere along his demented wanderings, had actually saved his life. For when a roving band from the Turkish Army found him, they attributed his desertion to illness. They shipped him home to where his mother nursed him back to health. But despite the restored health of his body, he knew the state of his mind was even worse than the sick body of the girl before him.

Deep lines creased his forehead as he watched her. Her breathing came ragged and rapid, and her skin appeared pallid as her body struggled to heal itself. A wave of compassion flooded over him. Yet another wave quickly followed and overcame him—one of anger—when he considered that such a fragile creature as this slight girl should have experienced such pain.

He felt quite certain he knew what had happened to her. Smyrna.

They had heard all sorts of conflicting press reports about what had been going on in that golden city before their ship had set sail. Many news reports had said his countrymen had gently retaken control of the city. But a smoky haze had risen from the metropolis, like a towering mountain extending thousands of feet into the sky. A fiery glow had been visible from their ship even during the daylight hours. And the girl they had found was a living testimony to an entirely different story. Often, he had heard the girl cry out in her uneasy sleep, "*fotia*," the Greek word for fire. Auhan knew without being told that the thick haze and red glow they had seen had caused the devouring of the buildings, the vegetation, the people, the animals of that great city. He looked down at the dog by the girl's feet.

Again the image of the grave pressed itself into his brain. One image in particular he could not shake—the sight of a little baby still wearing a sweater knitted from soft blue wool. The image tormented him every night. And haunted his every waking moment. Without a miracle, he doubted it would ever cease. And since Auhan didn't believe in the Almighty's goodness, he knew he could never expect such a thing.

He shook his head. He didn't realize how vigorously until the dog lifted his own head to regard him with a wary eye.

"It's okay, Boy," Auhan said. But the dog didn't seem reassured. With his mouth closed, he maintained a steady and tight gaze to watch Auhan.

They continued their stare-down for a few heartbeats until finally a ghost of a smile touched Auhan's lips. It was the first one in over a year.

"What's your story, Boy? You love her, don't you?" He stated the obvious as he motioned to the girl.

The sound of his voice seemed to, at last, reassure the animal. Giving a great big yawn, the golden beast lowered his head to the girl's feet once again, and his eyes slowly closed.

Looking at the dog, Auhan sighed. He had forgotten how nice it felt to talk to the creatures, even if in secret, as he had his father's farm dog. He expelled a deep breath. The fact that he had always had to hide his love of dogs was just one more thing in a long list of things that bothered Auhan. All the rules and regulations, the dos and don'ts in life. And for what? To placate an Almighty who didn't care?

Covering his face with his hands, Auhan rubbed his fingers over his eyes. An old, familiar heaviness pressed on his chest and nearly cut off his breathing whenever he thought too much, too deeply.

How Auhan wished he could start life all over again. To go back into his mother's womb and be born an innocent little baby right now—today—and not have to deal with all the emotions that tugged and pulled at him so hard and made it difficult to draw air into his lungs.

He wished to not only start a new life in a new land but to be *totally* reborn.

He heaved a shaky sigh.

But he knew it was only a wish. A senseless wish. A little child's daydream. Reality was his life with its knowledge of the evil doings in the world; reality was the war being fought daily within his mind; reality was never being able to truly start life all over again—even in a new land, in America.

At twenty, Auhan, with the burden of knowledge, of knowing evil, of having met it face-to-face at the mass Christian grave, felt older than time itself.

Bitterness splintered through him. Why had he been forced to learn just how evil man could be? Why had he needed to learn about evil, period? Why?

He lowered his hands from his over eyes and sat back. A choking tightness wound itself deep inside him. With sweat beading upon his forehead, upon his chest, and even upon his back, he forced himself to stop thinking.

To stop.

Stop.

Glancing at his father's timepiece, he saw it was time to

get more liquid into the girl. She also had a definite war waging within her. A physical one.

He reached for the spoon. Then, taking care not to touch her numerous burns, he gently lifted her dainty head. He poured the healing liquid past her cracked and bruised lips and down her throat. The back of her neck was hot, so hot it burned against his fingertips in an unnatural way. She moaned slightly in protest to the hurting movement, and yet her tongue moved around her mouth, and she did all she could to work the soup into her system.

Auhan recognized in her a will to live as strong as any he had ever seen. He had no such will last year when he had been so gravely ill. It had been his mother's will that had made him physically well again. But he was convinced. If this girl hadn't possessed her own fierce will to live, she would have succumbed to the sea long before being rescued.

On that fateful evening, he had been standing out on deck regarding the infinite stars when the dolphins started jumping up and down and all around. The sailors trained a light down upon them and discovered the girl and the dog in the middle of the cavorting, dancing dolphins. The sight was one of the most amazing things those hardened sailors and he had ever experienced. Auhan knew he would never forget the sight even if he should live to the turning of the next century, which was something he didn't expect. As she and the dog clung to each other, she had looked so small, so vulnerable, and yet somehow strong too.

The captain, seamen, and the few passengers aboard the cargo ship all decided the girl's spirit must contain a matchless quality. In order for the dolphins to have responded to the girl and come to her rescue in such a magnificent way, the innocent creatures must have recognized something very, very special about her.

Auhan held to such a belief, and, therefore, he wasn't surprised to see that the more time he spent around her, the more she intrigued him. He understood why it might be so. Nevertheless, the feeling caught him off-guard. He couldn't even remember the last time someone had been able to arouse his attention. It felt strange, like a long-unused muscle being utilized again. Yet, it also felt good.

Still. . .dolphins coming to a person's aid? A dog for a companion in the choppy sea? Such things didn't happen every day, and only a dead person could ignore such an occurrence.

A humorless sound, a distant cousin to a laugh, escaped him. Throughout the previous long months, he had considered himself as good as dead. Her coming and proving him otherwise was both an unexpected and a welcome gift.

Bending a little bit closer, he studied her closed eyes. He wondered about their color and finally decided that they could either be blue like a sapphire or brown with bits of golden light to match her hair. And her name—Auhan wondered about that too.

Amazed by his pleasant thoughts, encouraged by them, he exhaled with a deep whoosh and glanced back at his mother. He had fed the girl ten times, and still his mother slept, safe in the arms of his father.

Auhan would not awaken her.

Even when, after a few minutes, chills started to course through the girl's body, Auhan decided against rousing his mother. He would follow his mother's way, and, as if he were a doctor or a nurse, he would care for the girl. As he lifted the spare blanket over the girl's shivering body and gently, yet vigorously, rubbed her slender limbs to help warm them, he was amazed to realize he really wanted to help—and not just for his mother's sake.

The dog, seeming to understand the girl's need for warmth,

inched his way up against her side. Auhan smiled at him. The dog blinked back, then placing his paws against the girl's arms, he sat and looked at her in loving concentration. To Auhan, the animal seemed to almost will his sea companion to open her eyes. He understood. He too wished the "Dolphin Girl" would awaken.

And open her eyes she did. The very next morning.

three

Likewise the Spirit also helpeth our infirmities:
for we know not what we should pray for as we ought:
but the Spirit itself maketh intercession for us with
groanings which cannot be uttered.
Romans 8:26

With clouded vision, Elena regarded the woman before her. This wasn't her very own mother, as her unconscious brain had falsely registered. Yet, the truth didn't diminish the beauty of the slender woman who stood above her, beaming with love.

"Dear girl." The woman ran her soft touch over the uninjured part of Elena's forehead. "Welcome back."

Elena blinked to clear her blurred eyes. She moved her parched and numb lips into a smile. Her mouth hurt. Every square inch of her body ached. And she felt utterly exhausted. But before sleep could capture her once again, she had to thank the woman for her care. Elena suspected that she had long been tending to her needs.

"Thank you," she whispered in Turkish, glad her brain had registered the fact that the people around her spoke in that tongue. But even as unconsciousness moved upon her once again, Elena felt no fear. These people were not her enemies. They were her friends.

"Sleep, Daughter. Sleep," she heard the woman say, and Elena felt assured that these people were not just her friends, but her family now.

Watching from behind his mother's shoulders, Auhan startled at the stirring of a now unfamiliar emotion when the girl's eyelids suddenly parted. As he had suspected, her eyes were brown with golden pinpricks of light, which made his own widen as he gazed into them. A light emanated from her soul and filled the cabin with a joy he hadn't felt in years—since before the Great War. He couldn't help but wonder how brightly these eyes would sparkle when she was in better health. Perhaps they would be too brilliant for him to return a steady gaze.

"Her fever is down, praise God," Fatima exclaimed. The deep, even breathing of the girl indicated her improving health.

However, his mother's words sliced into the heart of Auhan's confusion like a knife does a loaf of bread. "Don't you mean, Allah?" he retorted at her use of the Almighty's title.

She had been using the Christian name, God, more than the Muslim's Allah since they boarded this American vessel. In truth, he liked neither name. To his way of thinking, his mother's work had healed the girl. Not an uncaring Almighty.

Slowly, Fatima turned her head. In the light coming through the portholes, the wisps of gray amid the dark hair escaping her scarf gleamed like platinum. She regarded him with such patience, a twinge of regret for his words seized Auhan.

"God," his mother answered with neither fear nor doubt creeping into her voice. Even as feelings of annoyance slashed through him, Auhan recognized this lack of fear had to be a heady feeling for his mother. She had grown up in a society that not only allowed but encouraged a fellow Muslim to kill a neighbor suspected of having Christian leanings. His mother had such leanings all of his life. Maybe even all of her own. She looked away from him and down at the girl again. "It is the God of Jesus Christ who has saved her," she declared with boldness.

Auhan sighed. That statement rankled and made his anger boil within him as fiercely as hurricanes do the Atlantic, the ocean they were soon to enter.

"It is *you* who has saved her, *Anne*," he corrected. "Neither God nor Allah—whichever name you choose—had *anything* to do with her being saved. And besides, how do you know for certain that she is a Christian?" Even to his own ears, he sounded like a child throwing a tantrum. "She just thanked you in Turkish."

"Many Greeks speak Turkish. And whenever she cries out, it is in the Greek language." Auhan knew his mother spoke the truth.

She reached into her pocket and drew out a pure white handkerchief, unfolding the cloth with reverent respect. The contents revealed from within the folds of the pure, white fabric made Auhan step back, almost as if he had been struck. His spirit had. Struck by the object in his mother's hand. An object he had never seen her hold before.

"I know because of this." She held up a cross that appeared to be both very old and, undoubtedly, extremely valuable. Precious jewels heavily studded the piece. "I found it sewn into her clothing."

Auhan looked between the girl and the ancient emblem of her belief. Had her God saved her from death in the rough sea? It was a nice thought. But he didn't give it more than half a second to sit in his brain before anger swooped in to replace it.

"The question should be, 'How come her God allowed her to even be in a situation of such danger in the first place?' " No. Auhan would not believe that God, as revealed by Jesus Christ, was any better than Allah, as revealed by the Koran.

In fact, the God of Jesus Christ seemed weaker. At least Allah was strong in war. His people weren't being killed in death marches or being fished from the sea as this girl had been. God, as represented by that cross, seemed to sit back and let others violate His people—men, women, children, *babies*—in the worse possible way. And wasn't the Great War a case of Christian fighting against Christian? What did that say?

The truth was, Auhan believed that neither God nor Allah cared for people. Auhan didn't care which interpretation of Him people used.

Evil was in charge of the world.

Not God.

Not Allah.

Not an Almighty.

He looked at the cross again and then at his mother. His very tired mother. Out of three children, the woman had only one child left—one very bitter, very angry, very confused child. Auhan knew that she held hopes that his brother still lived. But that was a hope Auhan didn't share with her. After all, why would Allah allow his mother's oldest son to live if he hadn't allowed her only daughter the same privilege? And, at the moment, his mother was also homeless. Her home was this room on this rolling little steamship in the middle of this big sea.

Yet even as he thought about their homelessness, Auhan knew it to be something good. He believed his parents had made the correct decision in leaving their home. Who knew what plans the politicians were cooking up for the people in their area of the world this year—both Turkish and Greek? At least now they were still able to emigrate to America.

Auhan had a feeling that soon the gates to that golden land would be closed. His mother could not have taken such news at this point in her life. She had dreamt of going to America for as long as he could remember and had worked toward it just as long. His family would not be arriving in the New World as paupers.

"Auhan." He heard her call his name and realized he had been staring at her. He blinked his eyes and looked at her again, really focusing on her this time. Remorse filled him to see the deep lines of concern etched in her classically pretty face—concern he knew he had placed there.

"I'm sorry, *Anne*. Don't worry." The shadow of a smile touched his lips. "I will be fine." He wasn't sure his assurances were true, but he wouldn't add to either of his parents' anxieties by saying otherwise. He glanced at his father, who, in his normal way, had been silently observing everything.

"I *do* worry, my son," his mother insisted as she wrapped the cross in the fine cloth and placed it back into the pocket of her dress. She just managed to complete the task before the boat dropped sharply on a wave. Auhan reached out for her elbow, but his steadying hand was unnecessary. His mother had already caught herself and adjusted to the rolling of the Mediterranean Sea. Both he and his mother had discovered themselves to be true seamen on this trip.

He let go of her, and he braced his feet farther apart to counter the motion of the ship. He wanted to explain. He owed her that much and so much more.

"What I'm feeling inside, *Anne*," he touched his hand to his forehead, "is dark and gray and ugly—something only *I* can push out of me. I'm not sure that I will ever be able to—" He licked his lips as he watched her eyes fill with tears. This was the very reason he hadn't told her his feelings before. He felt horrible about making his strong mother cry.

"But, *Anne*," he sighed out, and glanced back at his father to include him, "*Baba*, I promise you both that I *will* try." He paused. "I am trying."

He startled to discover the absolute truth of the declaration.

He hadn't realized his intentions until that moment. But since the girl had come to be with them, he had been trying.

Auhan didn't want to be a zombie. But if he didn't allow himself to think, then the little baby in the blue sweater could not haunt his mind—at least, not as easily. Yet since the "Dolphin Girl" had come, he *was* thinking again and, sometimes, even thinking nice thoughts. He didn't know why the girl should make such a difference to him. He just knew for some reason she had.

His mother took a deep breath. "I believe you, my son." She reached up and pulled him down to her level in order to kiss the right and left points of his forehead, something she had done for as long as he could remember. Then, she stood back, and, blinking tears from her clear, green eyes, she regarded him with such an intensity that he stood a little taller.

"I also believe two other things. First, that this move to America will be partly responsible for saving you." He could tell from the way she paused, with an expectant tilt to her head, that she had been nearly certain that he would refute her observation.

He didn't. How could he? He too suspected their moving away from the old, war-torn land and starting fresh in the new would help him. Already, just being on the ship had helped. He had discovered a real love for sea travel. That and the girl proved to be two good reasons to get up every day. Before leaving home, there had been times when he hadn't left his bed or his shuttered room for days.

When he didn't make a comment, his mother continued. "Second—" She looked away from him and placed her hand across the sleeping girl's cheek. "I believe this girl—and her God—will fill the part of you that the move doesn't. There is light in her." She turned back to Auhan. "A light you need, my son."

A light he needed? Auhan wanted to scoff at his mother's proclamation. He knew he would have if he hadn't already challenged her. He felt guilty about doing so again.

But he watched the sleeping girl carefully during the next couple of days. He couldn't deny the joy she brought to their little world every time she awoke. His mother seemed happier, as did his father. And yes, even he.

Here the girl lay, sick and bruised, far from everyone she knew, and yet she had a strength about her, an inner radiance, that both astounded and mesmerized Auhan. Despite his resolve not to, he found himself waiting for the moments when she opened her eyes. He didn't try to analyze why. But he knew somehow, even in her weakened state, she was transforming his feelings of despair.

Each time he gazed into her eyes he felt a stirring within his soul, as if a spark were trying to ignite—to find life. For the first time since he had discovered the mass grave, Auhan found himself truly interested in someone.

With the first fluttering of her lids, his pulse jumped to a quicker beat. He watched as her gaze would first search out his mother, smile at her; then search out his father, smile at him; and then look for him.

She would smile, and he would smile back. Always. With not just a little turning up of his lips but a great big, broad grin. Then, his mother's eyes would dance in delight, and his father would chuckle in mirth as he had long ago, when the daughter of his own body had been alive.

Auhan knew his mother had been correct. Even with all the "Dolphin Girl" had been through, she illuminated the world around her. The darkness that had settled upon his soul the previous year was now not as great because of her. And when the girl laid her hand upon the dog's head, as she always did before allowing her eyes to close in sleep, Auhan couldn't help but wonder from where her strength came.

The image of the cross his mother carried in her pocket flashed into his mind. He knew she still carried it because he had seen her take it out several times and look at it in a longing way. Was that cross—what it stood for—the source of the girl's strength, her happiness? Had Jesus actually been more than just a prophet? Contrary to what the Koran wrote about Jesus in Sura al-Nisa' 4:157, "They crucified him not," had Jesus, in truth, died on the cross only to live again? Could He truly be God's Son?

Auhan shook his head. He was so confused. Once again, he wished he could talk over such things with his brother. He missed Mehmet fiercely. Of the two, Mehmet was the thinker, but he had always challenged his younger brother to do the same.

Before coming across the mass grave, Auhan had been a deeper thinker than most of his friends. But he hadn't allowed himself to dwell on such contemplations for such a long time now. Somehow, though, he knew that he was coming to the point where he would have to face his beliefs—or lack thereof—directly. They were, after all, sailing to a new land, a place where a person was allowed to think and believe what they wanted without fear. But did he really want to think that much? Would the little baby in the blue sweater allow him the freedom of such thought?

Every time the girl awoke, she left something behind. Something elusive but something right and true. Lovely and pure. A feeling that reached deep down inside of him and quickened his soul—much akin to the feeling he used to get when he played his violin. Only better. Much better. Her very eyes possessed a wonderful ability to scatter joy all around her.

❧

Elena remained too weak to manage more than the "thank

you" she had uttered the first day she opened her eyes, but she wasn't too weak to pray for the wonderful people who had taken her in. She prayed that the Lord would work in their lives in His own glorious way and bring peace and grace to their souls—particularly to the young man.

Something about him seemed familiar to Elena, although she couldn't place what it was. She certainly sensed he was hurting. His eyes reflected a pain much deeper than the physical pain that racked her body. Her body would recover with care and time. Yet, Elena sensed that the young man's hurt was a spiritual pain, a pain only God could heal.

Elena feared the young man would never find peace without the direct intervention of Jesus.

four

*"For false Christs and false prophets shall rise,
and shall shew signs and wonders, to seduce,
if it were possible, even the elect."*
Mark 13:22

When Elena awoke early the next day, she felt a fresh physical energy flowing through her. Although her muscles still hurt fiercely, the general ache of fever no longer compounded her body's pain. Her throbbing headache had disappeared. Her head felt heavy but not in an aching way. She looked over at the dog sleeping by her side. Her fingers slowly uncurled, and she rubbed his golden fur.

The dog lifted his great head, and his soft brown gaze met hers. As they had when in the sea, woman and dog looked lovingly at one another.

"Dear Buddy," Elena croaked out after several minutes had passed, with a voice that seemed very foreign to her. "We made it, Boy. We made it." He nudged her hand in reply, and she patted his snout as tears of happiness slid from the corners of her eyes. "Thank you for keeping me company in the sea, Buddy. I don't think that I could have survived without you." He rewarded her words of gratitude with a gentle thump of his tail and the dearest doggie grin she had ever seen. Her smile deepened, and she realized her lips no longer hurt. As she moistened her lips with her tongue, she could still feel scabs, yet they didn't pull as before.

With expectancy for the new day, she turned her head

toward the porthole. But the color filtering through the window was not the blue she had anticipated. Rather the light glowed red, like the red of Smyrna burning. Like her father's blood. Sad tears flowed from her eyes while she whimpered, "*Baba.*"

And again.

"*Baba. . .*"

At her outcry, the young man who had been dozing in a chair near her bed moved quickly to her side. His gaze flicked between her and the red sky beyond the porthole. "It's okay. It's just the sunrise," he said, patting her shoulder.

"It's just. . .so. . .red," she whispered. She covered her eyes with her hand in an attempt to block the terrifying color of glowing fire from her view.

"Soon it will be blue," he assured her. At his words, she lowered her hand to look at him and found comfort in his smiling face. "Here." He slipped a hand under her head to gently lift her up. "Since you're awake, please have a sip of broth." He brought the cup to her lips with his other hand. She did as he instructed and drank heartily in an effort to quench her never-ending thirst.

Rather than dwelling on her thoughts of Smyrna, she forced herself to concentrate on his hands as they held the cup. They looked like the hands of an aristocrat—long and slender with clean and trim nails. Elena had seen someone else with such hands recently. But the memory of exactly where was trapped somewhere within her brain.

"How are you feeling?" He moved the cup away from her lips and placed it on the table behind her head.

"Much better." She gave him the most encouraging smile she could muster. Yellow sunlight now bathed the cabin, and Elena studied the kind stranger. He looked every bit as handsome as Elena's muddled brain had registered during the previous days of semiconsciousness. His high forehead matched the nobility of his hands. But along with his good looks and slender build, she noticed his brooding quality, sensed his uneasy mind. Visible not only in his dark eyes, the cloud of grief seemed to wrap around his entire body. She wondered what had happened to place such sorrow there.

"What's your name?" he asked softly. She noted he was unable to meet her gaze as he spoke. He looked at the dog instead.

"Elena," she responded.

"Elena," he echoed. "Your name means 'light.' "

"I like the way you say it," she said, surprising herself with her own straightforwardness. "And your name is?"

"Auhan."

She nodded her head. Now she had a name to use when praying. "Thank you, Auhan, for caring for me."

He motioned to the bunk where an older couple slept. "It was my mother who nursed you. She didn't leave your side for days."

Days? How many? She frowned, and the motion made her forehead sting. She reached up with her right hand to explore her face but stopped when she noticed, for the first time, the bandage wrapped around the back of her hand. She raised her left hand. She was perplexed to see bandages encasing it too. Only a portion of her fingers protruded from the dressing. Then, she remembered. The fire falling from the sky. The burning of her skin. Her father dying. The bitter memories engulfed her, and her eyes closed as an involuntary quiver shook her body.

"Elena. . ." Auhan stroked her uninjured fingers.

The sound of his voice and the feel of his fingers around her own were like lifelines to her. She forced her eyes to open and to look into his.

From the language he spoke she knew he was Turkish. All human reasoning told her that she should hate him because of that fact. His race had destroyed her city, killed her father, separated her from her sisters.

But human reasoning didn't rule Elena. God ruled her. Neither this man nor his parents were to blame for what had happened to her and her family—to all the Christians in Smyrna. This Turkish family had been a blessing to her, not a bane.

"Do you want to tell me about it?" Auhan prompted her with a comforting half-whisper, and she slowly nodded her head. She did want to talk about it. All of the happenings in Smyrna had been roaming around her subconscious for days, and somehow she knew that she had to get them out. But she worried she was not yet strong enough. Perhaps she needed a few more days of rest before telling the ugly tale. Before telling about the evil that had invaded the streets of her city.

"Auhan." Sleepiness tinged the voice of the woman on the cot as she spoke. "Is she okay?"

Auhan smiled back at his mother. "*Anne*. I'd like for you to meet Elena. Elena, may I introduce my *Anne*, Fatima."

"Oh!" the older woman exclaimed as she quickly scrambled out of bed and across the space of the small room. The smile she leveled down at her seemed so familiar to Elena. "Dear girl," she breathed out, and Elena watched in amazement as her deep, green eyes filled with tears of happy relief.

When the other woman reached out her hand and brushed it against her cheek, Elena's eyes briefly closed at the wonderful and familiar touch. "Finally, your fever is totally gone! You are better!"

Elena smiled up at her. "Much better, *Anne* Fatima." She used the Turkish word for "mother," which Elena could see pleased the woman very much. "Thanks to you."

Fatima shook her head, and Elena watched in question as she dug deeply into the pocket of her dressing gown for something. "No. It is thanks to God that you are well." She held up the cross.

Elena gasped as she recognized it. "My mother's cross. . . the one. . . I had sewn into my dress. . ." She looked from the woman to her son, whose hand still covered her fingers. The woman gave the credit of her recovery to God. And she was holding up the cross.

Elena wiggled the fingers of her free hand through the dog's fur. They had also allowed Buddy to stay with her, not only in this cabin, but also on her bed, something she knew a Muslim family would never condone. Did that mean that this family was a rarely heard of Turkish Christian family? Elena had to know.

"Are you. . ." She paused and looked between the mother and son and the older man who sat on the far bunk. "I mean, do you believe in Jesus Christ?"

A shadow seemed to cross Fatima's face, and Elena felt the blood rush to her own face at having asked such a personal question of people who were, in truth, still strangers to her. But as the woman spoke, Elena's regret evaporated like fog touched by the rays of the sun.

"I'm not proud to admit this," Fatima began, "but our ancestry is that of apostatized Christians. The people of our bloodline renounced Jesus Christ in order to live in their homes without the terrible discriminations, including the dreaded blood tribute of earlier years, imposed upon Christians by the Ottoman Empire."

Elena knew she referred to the hundreds of years when agents of the sultan had combed the empire for the ablest Christian boys between the ages of ten and twelve. Those boys found to be of top physical and mental quality had been taken from their family, forcibly converted to Islam, and made into the elite fighting corps of the sultan, the Janissary corps. The boys were never to be seen by their families again—except as adversaries sent to kill the very ones who had given them life, their Christian parents. In the face of this terrible crime against humanity, Elena marveled that throughout the middle and late medieval ages so many Greeks, Armenians, and other Christians hadn't apostatized after finding their homeland under the rule of the nomadic conquerors, the Seljuk and Ottoman Turks from the steppes of Asia. Most modern Christians would agree—to have one's child taken because of the "crime" of being a believer would be even harder than giving one's own life for one's faith. Elena wasn't a mother yet, but she was sure this must be so.

"However," Fatima continued after a lengthy pause, her voice barely above a whisper, "I would like. . .to find. . .the God of my ancestors once again." Elena, seeing how Fatima rubbed the cross between her fingers, regarded her with curiosity. Such soft words, so few, and yet words that Elena knew had the ability to change the dear woman's entire life. Wonder filled Elena as, letting go of Auhan's hand, she reached out and placed her fingers over Fatima's, which now held tightly to the cross, the cross of Jesus Christ. "He's so easy to find, *Anne* Fatima. So easy."

Fatima carefully covered Elena's wounded hand with her other one and lowered herself to the side of Elena's bed. "When you are well," she implored, her green eyes intense with longing, "would you help me?"

Making a little half laugh, half cry sound, but which equaled total happiness, Elena sent up a silent prayer to God for Him having literally washed her into the path of this wonderful, searching woman. "It would be my greatest delight, *Anne* Fatima," Elena responded truthfully, and, reaching up, she wrapped her arms around the slender woman's shoulders in her famous, impromptu hug.

ᴥ

Watching as the two women held one another close, Auhan thought that not only their eyes but their entire bodies seemed to radiate a golden joy.

But joy wasn't what Auhan was feeling, golden or otherwise. Anger, confusion, and a multitude of emotions he couldn't even begin to identify battled within him like a skirmish full of ricocheting bullets. His fingers, his now empty fingers, clenched into a fist.

When Elena had let go of his hand to touch the cross in his mother's hand, he had felt as though he had been cast out into the darkest night and exchanged for something, or Someone, who didn't care as much as he was beginning to. But despite the blood that surged and pounded like the ocean within his head, he forced himself to calm down and to think.

What exactly did his mother mean by saying that she wanted to "find" the God of her ancestors? That was something Auhan had never heard before, and annoyance flickered through his thoughts. Did his mother really believe there was much of a difference between the two religions? Was she planning on exchanging one impotent way of regarding the Almighty for another?

Auhan looked between the two women. They seemed to be communicating on a different plane, one on which he didn't belong. His mother looked happy. Yet, her happiness went beyond that of human control to a realm that was, for him, very suspect.

Hearing his father arise from his bunk, Auhan glanced his way. But the older man was watching his wife. Auhan saw a smile curve his father's lips beneath his thick mustache. Judging from the glint in his eyes, his father found pleasure at the sight of his happy wife.

Auhan wished he felt the same way. He just didn't. He couldn't believe he could trust his mother's source of joy. Then again, Auhan didn't believe there was anything in this evil world that he *could* trust.

His mother might be happy today, but what about tomorrow? Had they so quickly forgotten Elena had been fished from the sea only a few days before? Where had the God of Jesus Christ been then?

Probably off in the same place He had been when the baby—the Christian baby—in the blue sweater had been thrown into that mass grave, Auhan thought as seeds of anger flowered within him. The walls of the cabin seemed to press upon him, and Auhan knew he had to get out.

"Excuse me," he said, a metallic quality lacing his voice. He grabbed his cap and motioned to the dog to follow him out of the room.

From his peripheral vision he caught a glimpse of his mother's eyebrows arching upward. He knew she was surprised by his abrupt departure. Yet, he also knew her to be a very wise woman. Unlike most mothers, she wouldn't challenge him. And now, more than ever, he appreciated her for it.

As his feet clanged through the hollow passageway and the paws of his companion tapped behind him, Auhan continued to ponder his mother's declaration. To believe in God as revealed by Jesus Christ was, in Auhan's opinion, an even weaker alternative than to believe in Allah as revealed by the Koran. To believe in Allah at least didn't require much thought. No one had to "find" Allah. They just had to follow the rules. Belief in Jesus required too much on the part of humans. *And for what?* Auhan wondered as he swung open the deck's door. *To be forgotten when evil reared its ugly face?*

The ocean wind pushed at Auhan when he stepped out

onto the middle deck, and sea spray washed over him. He stood still and filled his lungs with fresh air. He liked the feel of the spray upon his face—as if it washed him clean each time he stepped into its path.

Walking over to the railing, his hand idly stroked the dog's head, and he gazed out over the sea and sky. Regarding the unbroken seascape made him feel free. The way music once made him feel.

For music resounded from the sea.

Carried on the wind.

Singing not in billowing voices of nature's grandeur but in whispers. Gentle murmurs upon his soul.

Auhan filled his lungs with a deep, rejuvenating breath. He liked to stand on the deck. He could breathe deeply there. Surrounded by the unbridled, expansive sea, he could almost live with himself.

five

"Where is this ship heading?" Elena asked as she ate the soft-boiled egg that Fatima patiently spooned into her mouth. Elena felt stronger and stronger by the hour and now even sat up in bed.

"To America," Fatima responded, and Elena's eyes widened.

Home. Feelings of excitement bubbled up as her gaze skidded over to the porthole.

She was going home. To the land of her birth. The miracle of God's provision caressed her mind like a soft ocean breeze would her skin.

"America," she breathed as she studied Auhan's face. He sat on the opposite bunk. "But how—?" she asked. The Italian rescue ship had been taking the refugees from Smyrna only as far as Athens's port of Piraeus.

"Don't worry, Elena," Auhan answered her quickly, motioning to his father sitting beside him and to his mother before her. "My parents have already agreed. If you are amenable to the idea, they will adopt you. They have all the necessary papers to enter America, and as their daughter you will not be turned away."

Elena's eyes sought out Auhan's parents. With big smiles covering their faces, the older couple nodded their agreement. Their generous offer touched a cord deep within

59

Elena's heart, and, as a slow smile moved across her face, she whispered up yet another prayer of thanksgiving to God for bringing her to these wonderful people.

"I thank you." Emotion made her tone husky. "That is one of the nicest things anyone has ever offered to do for me." She reached out and touched both of their hands in turn. "Since my parents are now both gone from this earth, I would count it an honor and a privilege to be known as your daughter. But," she said with a shrug of her shoulders, "you don't have to do so in order to get me into the United States." She paused, then declared in perfect English, "I am American."

"What?" Fatima's mouth dropped open while Auhan's eyes widened momentarily, then narrowed.

"You. . .are. . .American?" he asked in broken English. His parents had taught themselves and both he and his brother to write in English. They could read almost anything and possessed extensive vocabularies. But neither he nor his parents had heard the language spoken by a native speaker before boarding the *Ionian Star,* where they heard the seamen speak it. To hear Elena speak English—and those particular English words—stunned him. The ramifications behind her pronouncement were huge.

With her eyebrows rising slightly, Elena nodded her head, confirming her proclamation.

"Then what were you doing adrift in the Aegean Sea?" Auhan asked with a caustic tone in his voice.

"Although my mother was American, my father. . .was. . . ," Elena stuttered over her first past tense reference to her father. "He was. . .a Greek man. From Smyrna."

Fatima thumped the bowl with the egg onto the table and Elena jumped at the clatter. If *Anne* Fatima hadn't immediately reached for her fingers and squeezed them in a comforting way, Elena would have worried that the other woman disliked hearing she was part Greek.

"You often screamed out for your *Baba*—your father—in your sleep." Fatima stroked her hair. "And for ones called Sophia, Rose, and Christos. Who are they?"

Elena tipped her head downward slightly. Elena recognized the time had come for her to address some important issues. "Sophia is my older sister. Since my mother died when I was but a child, Sophia and I have always been particularly close. Rose is my informally adopted little sister. Sophia and I took her in when her parents were killed, at the same time our father was shot. . .the last night. . .we were in Smyrna," she explained and squeezed her eyes shut as the image of that horrible moment on the quay swooped in on her. She could feel the blood drain from her face and felt her lips start to tremble, but at the pressure of Fatima's fingers on her own, she opened her eyes and looked into the loving eyes of the woman who had nursed her back to health.

"We are very sorry to hear about your father," Fatima murmured her condolences. "But you must not think of such sad things. You are not strong enough. You must think of only good things, good memories with your father. Tell us only if your sisters and the one called Christos yet live, and then we will ask no more." She flashed Auhan a mother's look of admonishment before returning her gaze to Elena.

Elena knew *Anne* Fatima was right. She could not dwell on her father's death. Her father's physical life, as she knew it, was gone. Yet, the spirit that had made him Andreas Apostologlou still lived. Elena knew with certainty she would meet him again someday. And on that day, he would have a brand new body. One unmarred by bullets.

"Thank you, *Anne* Fatima." She squeezed the other woman's fingers as much as her injured ones allowed. "I will only think of things that help me to get well." As she had done her entire life, Elena resolved to give all bad thoughts to God.

"Good." Fatima smiled and nodded for her to continue.

"Yes. My sisters and Christos live. We were rescued from the sea by a very overcrowded Italian ship. I was sleeping against the edge when I—" She grimaced at the thought. "—I, quite literally, fell overboard. That's how I ended up in the Aegean Sea."

"Why didn't the ship come back for you?" Auhan asked in a judgmental tone.

She shook her head vehemently to dispel any suspicions that someone from the ship was at fault. "No one saw me fall. Most likely, by the time my sisters or Christos even discovered that I was missing, the ship had steamed miles away."

"And who is this Christos?" Auhan asked. If Elena didn't know better, she would have suspected a jealous motive behind the question.

"Christos is a Greek soldier whom Sophia and I had met only a few days before." She paused and had to think exactly when it was. "The Thursday before the Turkish soldiers. . ." Remembering her audience, she stumbled on her words. But at their looks of encouragement, she continued, "before the Turkish soldiers entered the city. Christos had carried a wounded soldier from the battlefields all the way to our doorstep. He left him with us to care for him." She remembered back to that day, the last day Smyrna had been. . .Smyrna.

"Christos wouldn't even come in to rest. His only concern was for his friend. But something happened between my sister and Christos." Elena thought she could see a noticeable easing of Auhan's shoulders as he drew a deep breath.

"They hardly exchanged words before he shuffled away, but they definitely experienced a strong emotional exchange. And, when we met again the following Wednesday—"

"But how did you meet up with him again on Wednesday?" Auhan interrupted. "I overheard before leaving port that all the Greek soldiers had left for Greece before the Turkish troops entered Smyrna."

Elena felt the need to cough, but she tried to suppress it. "I think Christos. . ." She paused and swallowed and prayed that she wouldn't cough. Once she started, she knew that she wouldn't be able to stop for several minutes, "He was the only. . ." she swallowed again and took a sip of her tea, "Greek soldier left," she finally answered, glad that, with the help of her soothing chamomile, she had avoided a coughing fit.

She explained how Christos had not only saved her and her sisters from a brutal attack outside their home when they had returned for their rowboat, but had, in fact, gotten them and the other women and children who had occupied their rowboat aboard the Italian ship in the harbor. "We all owe our lives to Christos. From the soldier he carried to our home—who was Turkish, by the way—"

"Turkish?" Auhan interrupted and made a disagreeable sound. "A Greek helping a Turk?" he challenged, with thinned lips.

Elena's eyes flashed. "Tell me, Auhan," she responded without allowing even a breath to intervene. "Is it any stranger than a family of Turks helping a Greek?" She held out her hand to indicate the three of them.

She patted her chest with her bandaged hand. "I am American, but I am Greek too. Both facts of which I am very proud." Elena always had been. She was a product of the oldest democratic nation in the world and one of the newest and best, a position she knew was very unique. And, both modern countries—the USA and Greece—had always been allies—a very special relationship that very few countries in the world today could claim. If Auhan wanted to take issue with her dual nationalities, she knew it was better for him to do so now rather than later.

Elena watched as Auhan's jaw hardened in defiance, but after a moment he expelled his held breath and sent her a half smile. She returned it with a full one of her own.

In that instant, something happened between them. A spark. A sigh. Something as exciting as a festive summer fair and as calm as a good book read together by the fireplace on a cold winter's night. A nice feeling that seemed to soften Auhan's heart as much as her own.

"I suppose you are right," he finally admitted. "This Christos carrying the Turkish soldier to safety is not really any different than our caring for you."

"Besides," Elena continued after a moment, "I think that Christos would help anybody in the world in need. He didn't consider that man his enemy. In fact, they were friends. Christos is truly a man of God." She noted the slight stiffening of Auhan's spine at her declaration. "And someday," she hurried her words and turned to stare, unseeing, out the porthole, "I think that he's going to be my brother-in-law. He and my sister, they had only just met, but you know, love does come quickly under such extraordinary circumstances."

"I can see how that might happen," Fatima interjected. When Elena turned back toward her, she discovered *Anne* Fatima studying her and Auhan. The mother visibly bit the inside of her cheek while a slow, mischievous smile creased her cheeks. Fatima reached for the egg and spooned a little bit more into Elena's mouth. "So you will meet up with your sisters and Christos again soon."

❧

His mother spoke in the encouraging way of all mothers, but Auhan wondered just *how* they might find each other. Even so, he kept his questions to himself. Elena was still much too weak to consider such a task. Auhan knew, though, for family members to locate one another after a political separation could prove to be a difficult feat to accomplish and sometimes took years—if ever. He was glad that his parents had the foresight to set up a rendezvous point in America in the eventuality that any of them should become separated. If by chance his brother still lived, at least he, as well as they, knew when and where to meet one another again. It was a date they would keep each year until they were reunited.

"But for now," he heard his mother continue, "you must sleep. We will talk more later," she said as she gave the last of the egg to Elena, and, removing the wool shawl from around Elena's shoulders, she proceeded to fix the covers around the girl's slender form.

"*Anne* is right," Auhan said, and getting up, he motioned for Buddy to follow him. "We will take a walk up on deck." But as he reached for his hat, he flashed Elena a smile. "Soon, I hope that you will be able to come with us."

Auhan couldn't help but think as he watched her, everything about her glowed golden. Her eyes. Her hair. Her skin. Her spirit. Golden and bright.

The idea of being out in the elements didn't seem to appeal to Elena at all. She snuggled deeper down into her covers in a protective way. "I trust that is so," she responded with only her head poking out of the blanket. "To sit on the deck of a ship and just watch the sky pass before me *used* to be one of my favorite things in the world to do, something I gladly did for hours."

"Really?" Her words caught Auhan's interest. An image popped into his mind of the two of them sitting up on deck watching the clouds skitter across the sky. He was surprised to realize how much he liked the idea.

Elena nodded her head. "Although, after my mother died, we lived primarily in Smyrna, my father never wanted us to lose contact with America as our home too, so he took Sophia and me to America every summer."

"An ocean crossing every year?" Auhan asked with raised brows. By the standards of their village, his family had been considered well off. Yet, this was the first voyage they had ever been able to afford. He watched with interest the changing expressions crossing Elena's face as she nodded.

"I love every aspect of sailing across the sea," she continued, remembering her journeys. "The sound of the engines." She cocked her head as if listening to the noise of the self-propelled ship beneath them. "The vibration." She motioned to the glass of water and the liquid that jumped lightly within it. "The wind in my hair, the sea spray on my face, the seagulls greeting a ship after crossing the ocean, the dolphins." She smiled, a poignant turning up of her lips in remembrance of the dolphins that had saved her. "But mostly," she looked in the direction of the porthole, "I just love watching the sky," she sighed, and pulling her arm out of the blanket, she reached out her hand to touch the cool glass of the window and the firmament beyond. "Not just the sun rising in the morning or setting in the evening," she qualified, "but any time of the day or night and in any weather. I could just sit and look at it forever." She sighed wistfully, and turning back to Auhan, she caught her breath at how his eyes looked as they regarded her.

Holding a usually absent sparkle, they gleamed down on her like polished stones. She realized that for the first time since they'd met, he looked genuinely happy about something. She felt special in an unfamiliar way. A womanly way. She had never cared about pleasing a man before. Yet, where Auhan was concerned, pleasing him mattered a great deal to her.

"Since this is my first voyage, I've only just discovered that I too like watching the ocean sky," he admitted. It thrilled her to know that they had something in common.

"Maybe," he paused, and the sweetest grin moved his lips before he ventured to ask, "maybe soon, when you are better, you might enjoy sitting on deck with me where we might regard the sea and the sky together?"

Elena's eyes widened and that unfamiliar, womanly feeling intensified. Was he asking her for a date? If so, Elena knew that the idea appealed to her. In spite of the brooding quality so often evident in him, there were other attributes about him, elusive, but things that she knew were good and true, to which her spirit responded. She sensed that many of his best traits were locked deep inside of him. A slow, returning smile curved her lips, and she prayed that she might help bring out those special traits. "That would be delightful," she replied, feeling more like her elegant sister, Sophia, responding to one of her many suitors, than herself.

Auhan's gaze stayed on her for a moment longer, probing, searching. Trying, Elena thought, to understand what this reaction between them was—something she herself couldn't quite understand. Then, with an almost self-conscious nod, he turned, and, with the dog at his heels, he left the room. For a long moment, Elena stared at the doorway in wonder over what was happening between herself and Auhan. *Anne* Fatima's softly spoken, "Thank you," broke the comfortable silence.

Hearing a catch in the dear woman's voice, Elena pulled her gaze toward *Anne* Fatima and away from the door where the dog and the man had just exited—the man who was quickly becoming very special to her.

"Thank you?" Elena asked, genuinely perplexed. "For what?"

"For coming to us."

Elena stilled the woman's hand in the motion of tucking her into bed. "Dear *Anne* Fatima. It is *I* who must thank *you*."

But Fatima shook her head in adamant denial. "No. You have brought healing to our lives. To the life of our child." She motioned over to her husband, who nodded his ever silent, ever watching, ever observant head in agreement. "Your God has," Fatima qualified fearlessly, and Elena closed her mouth on the argument she had been about to offer.

For Auhan's parents to see a difference in their son meant that God *was* working in his life. Her prayers *were* being answered. *Oh dear Lord,* Elena whispered within herself to the God whom she knew always heard. *Thank you. Thank you.*

"Please," *Anne* Fatima wore a pleading expression, "just keep praying to your God for our son."

Elena's eyes widened at how closely the dear woman's words echoed her own thoughts. "Always," she whispered as *Anne* Fatima's loving hands finished settling her down for a nap.

But just before sleep overtook her brain, Elena did what *Anne* Fatima asked and even more. *Please God,* she prayed, *please bring Auhan and his dear parents to You. I want them to know the fullness of life—both now and eternally—known only by those who know Your Son. In the name of Your precious Son, Jesus, I pray.*

Her prayer was a simple one, yet one with mighty implications. And with its "*Amen,*" Elena knew that she could sleep soundly.

God was, as always, in control.

six

Who is a liar but he that denieth that Jesus is the Christ?
He is antichrist, that denieth the Father and the Son.
1 John 2:22

The next day, Elena patted Buddy's clean, golden fur with the fingers of her right hand while she raked the fingers of her left hand through her own clean hair. *Anne* Fatima had surprised her by washing it for her earlier that morning. As she worked, she lamented about how miserable Elena must have felt at having her hair caked with salt from the sea. She had used a homemade shampoo scented with chamomile, which now fragranced the air around Elena like a refreshing spring breeze.

Although Elena still felt weak, she felt like a new person with her hair falling soft and shiny around her shoulders. When *Anne* Fatima, her work done, came up to the side of the bed, Elena smiled up at her as her right hand continued to caress Buddy. They were alone in the cabin.

"You love that dog, don't you?" Although she phrased it as a question, it was actually more of a statement.

"*Anne*, his coming to me in the sea was a miracle." Elena's reply held no hesitation as she reached for her teacup and took a sip of the golden liquid within. Ever since she had become strong enough to sit up in bed, there had been an ever present cup of chamomile next to her. She loved the herbal tea. With each sip she couldn't help but think how wonderful it would have been if someone had offered that drink when she had been adrift in the sea. The consumption of liquids was something Elena would never take for granted again. "Just when I didn't think that I could go on any longer alone," she continued, "God sent Buddy and the dolphin to me." Elena had already explained to them all how that had happened. "But I think that the dolphin coming to Buddy's aid and keeping him afloat in the choppy water before finding me was the greater miracle."

"Miracle," Fatima murmured in concurrence and pulled the cross, Elena's cross, out of her pocket. Because of its value, they had agreed she would hold it for safekeeping until Elena was strong enough to look after it herself. Of the numerous pieces of jewelry Elena had sewn into her clothing, only the cross and her mother's wedding ring set had been found when Fatima had washed out her tattered clothes. The rest were either on the charred streets of Smyrna or sitting at the bottom of the deep, blue sea.

Seating herself on the trunk next to Elena, Fatima seemed to study the cross before turning to Elena and, with hesitation, voiced a question. Elena could tell the thought had long been on the dear woman's mind. "How do you live, Elena, without grief overwhelming you?" she finally asked. "You lost so much, and yet," Fatima looked at her with true, open-minded inquiry in her sharp green eyes, "you are like a light to us all."

A quick smile spread across Elena's face as she reached over and took the older woman's hand in her own. Elena's thumb rubbed the soft flesh of the woman whom she had grown to love deeply, then she moved to touch the metal of the beautifully crafted cross now warmed by Fatima's touch. "Dear *Anne* Fatima, it is God who gives me the power to live. Whenever my problems start to overwhelm me, I immediately give them to Him." She had been constantly doing that in regard to her father's death, her separation from her sisters, and the death of her city, of Smyrna, since consciousness had returned to her.

Fatima's fine brows came together in a quizzical frown. "*Give* your problems to God?" She placed a marveling emphasis on the word "give."

Elena started to take a deep breath, but it made her cough, so instead she took a sip of her tea, then another, and another before placing her cup back on the chest beside her. She didn't want a coughing fit to interrupt her. "When God created us, *Anne,* He never intended for us to live life without Him. Through sending His Son, Jesus, to earth, God made it possible for us to have the relationship with Him He had meant for us to have from the very beginning."

"Jesus really is God's Son?"

"He is, indeed."

Fatima shook her head. "Islam, the religion my family has been following, teaches that although Jesus was a great prophet. . .He was not, however. . .God's Son and. . . ," Fatima looked down at the cross in her hand, "that He was neither killed. . .nor crucified."

"But He was," Elena refuted in a soft voice. She rubbed the cross—the oh-so-important reminder of the actual cross of Jesus—which was responsible for bringing all who made the choice to believe in God's redemptive work back into fellowship with Him.

"Jesus said He came not to be ministered unto, but to minister and to give His life as a ransom for many," she paraphrased the New Testament verse. "*Anne*, Jesus ransomed His life on that cross for you, for me, for all of us. That was the very reason for which He came into the world. Only by dying on the cross could He achieve ultimate victory for humans over sin, death, and Satan and bring us back into full fellowship with God. In this way, this most glorious and love-filled way, He—God—serves us."

Fatima's mouth quirked into a dry line. "We are taught to minister to Allah. We are his servants, and we should always submit to him."

Elena had never been happier that her father had insisted that she and Sophia memorize scripture verses than at this moment. Her fingers itched to pick up her dearly loved Bible and to flip through its much worn pages as she talked to Fatima.

But she couldn't. Her Bible, like so many other Bibles in Smyrna, along with thousands of illuminated Greek manuscripts and letters from the earliest days of Christianity, were now gone. Burned to ashes.

Asking the Holy Ghost to guide her words, Elena spoke. "The Apostle John, a man who was very close to Jesus, wrote, 'But as many as received him'—Jesus—," Elena qualified, " 'to them gave he power to become the sons of God, even to them that believe on his name.'"

"Sons?" Fatima questioned, tilting her scarf-covered head to the side.

"Sons," Elena affirmed. "And because of this, if we believe that Jesus is who He Himself said He is—God's Son—then we become, by adoption, God's children. Jesus, God's begotten Son, came to serve us. He came to break the chains of darkness, which would then enable us to live in the light of God's love once again. *Anne* Fatima, children are not their parents' servants, but rather their parents' joy."

Earlier, while she had been washing her hair, Fatima had told Elena how her two sons and her little daughter had been the joys of her life since the days of their births.

"Please tell me more," Fatima prompted a bit breathlessly, and Elena was glad to do so.

"Jesus is God, but scriptures tell us that He 'made himself of no reputation, and. . .was made in the likeness of men: And being found in fashion as a man, he humbled himself, and became obedient unto death, even the death of the cross,' " Elena repeated her favorite Bible verses, those found in the second chapter of Philippians.

She could never think of them or repeat them without chills of sublime wonder coursing from one shoulder blade to the other, especially when she spoke the next words. " 'Wherefore God also hath highly exalted him, and given him a name which is above every name: That at the name of Jesus every knee should bow, of things in heaven, and things in earth, and things under the earth; And that every tongue should confess that Jesus Christ is Lord, to the glory of God the Father.'"

"But, this is something I find very confusing."

Elena startled at the sound of Auhan's voice. She turned to look at him as he stood in the doorway with his father. She had been so intent on her conversation with *Anne* Fatima, she hadn't heard them return to the cabin.

He pulled his cap from his head as he continued. "My brother and I used to discuss such things. While some Muslims view the Trinity as a union between God and Mary giving birth to Jesus, I understand Christians worship three gods—the Father, and the Son, with the Holy Ghost—not Mary—being the third party. Am I right?"

Elena shook her head from side to side. "No, Auhan. We believe in one God. One perfect and indivisible God."

"But, Father, Son, and Holy Ghost." He shrugged his shoulders. "Aren't they three different persons?"

Even though Elena knew that the question was a hard one, one of the hardest, to answer, the fact that he was even asking sent tremors of hope coursing through her. Her father, in spite of war and discrimination, had possessed a heart full of love for his Muslim neighbors. He had often told her that a Muslim who submitted uncritically to the authority of the Islamic religion, a recited, dictated religion, would never be able to see the truth about Jesus. To think with the rational mind God gave to humans was the first step.

While Islam was characterized by submission to Allah and his commands—no questions asked—the Christian God trusted people to use the brain He, Himself, had put into their heads. Consequently, the Christian God, unlike the Muslim's Allah, didn't fear questions. Quite the contrary. God welcomed them.

Even though she knew Auhan didn't realize it, just his inquiry meant he had crossed the first and most difficult hurdle. As she answered him, hope filled her—hope for his eventual salvation and maybe even hope for a future together with him.

"Yes, three different persons, Auhan, but still, one God. A unity in a Trinity." She wanted to keep everything simple.

She knew a person trained in the Muslim faith found the triune nature of God something very difficult to grasp. But Elena, backed by nearly two thousand years of her ancestors' belief in the redemptive work of Christ on the cross, also understood that without the mediation of the Son of God, God the Father would have remained in isolated splendor, being too holy for sinful man to even approach. And, without the Holy Ghost living in the midst of His people and dwelling in the believer, man would have been left on his own to try and follow God's holy precepts, an impossible task.

Elena studied Auhan's face before plowing ahead, praying all the while for the right words to dispel his suspicions. "After Jesus died on the cross and was resurrected, just before He was taken up to heaven, He told His disciples, 'All power is given unto me in heaven and in earth. Go ye therefore, and teach all nations, baptizing them in the name of the Father, and of the Son, and of the Holy Ghost.' "

Although Auhan didn't offer a verbal response, she sensed a dubious air settling around him like a disagreeable cloud.

"Auhan, Jesus spoke of 'Father, Son, and Holy Ghost' together in one phrase to mean God—one God. But for now, the main thing you need to know and believe can be summed up in this one verse, 'For God so loved the world, that he gave his only begotten Son. . .' " Her voice faltered, and she stopped speaking at the remembrance of the last time she had heard those beautiful words of promise. Sophia had spoken them on the quay right after their father had gone on to Paradise. As Elena continued to say the verse in her mind, her voice merged with the echoed memory of her sister's recitation. " 'That whosoever believeth in him should not perish, but have. . .everlasting. . .life.' "

Once more, the glorious assurance of knowing her father wasn't gone from her forever—that he hadn't perished— filled Elena with an inexplicable joy.

She turned her head and looked out the window. Elena could never describe this sensation, yet she felt as if the very arms of God reached down from heaven and enfolded her soul within His protective grasp.

"Oh, my! Could it really be so very simple?" *Anne* Fatima exclaimed.

Elena turned to look at her, and the sight nearly left her breathless. Her eyes shone like emeralds washed by the sea. She seemed like a little girl opening the best present she could have ever imagined receiving. She was. The gift of salvation.

"That's basically it," Elena agreed, her voice tight with emotion. "But not only did He die for us, *Anne*, but He was resurrected as well. That's what Pascha, Easter, is all about. Jesus was killed; He was crucified, but after being dead for three days and in His tomb, He rose again to life. He didn't just ascend to heaven without dying on the cross as the Koran claims. Jesus was horribly tortured; He died—a historical fact witnessed by thousands—and three days later He rose again to life. Life! By doing all this not only did He mark the way for us back to God—Himself—but He conquered death for us too."

"And the Holy Ghost?" Fatima asked. "We have been taught that the Comforter whom Jesus referred to is the prophet Mohammed, and the Holy Ghost is the angel Gabriel who brought messages from God to both Mary and Mohammed."

This was not the first time Elena had heard about the Muslim belief that the Comforter was Mohammed and the Holy Ghost was someone other than God. But, as always, such false doctrine made chills run up and down her spine. From their childhood, so many people like Fatima had been falsely taught about the Holy Spirit. The Comforter and the Holy Ghost were One and the same—the very One who lives within a believer. For *Anne* Fatima to so misunderstand this fact truly saddened Elena.

Coughing in agitation over these troubling thoughts, Elena reached for her chamomile and took a sip before offering a gentle answer to her precious friend, again using the inspired words of the Bible. "Jesus said, 'I will pray the Father, and he shall give you another Comforter, that he may abide with you for ever; Even the Spirit of truth; whom the world cannot receive, because it seeth him not, neither knoweth him: but ye know him; for he dwelleth with you, and shall be in you. I will not leave you comfortless: I will come to you.' "

Anne Fatima looked as if a light had been turned on within her soul. She seemed to understand everything. However, Elena could tell Auhan was doubtful by the firm set of his jaw.

❧

In truth, it did indeed sound to Auhan as if the Counselor was the third person of the one God Elena described. Still, he just wasn't sure. No matter what his distant ancestors might have believed, he still wasn't even certain that he wanted to know more about God, Allah—Whomever. The Almighty was still pretty low on his list.

Even so, Elena's enthusiasm about the subject electrified the air. Her eyes seemed to sparkle with an inner fire. Sunbeams poured through the porthole and surrounded her hair with a halo of heavenly light. As Elena continued her treatise, Auhan knew she addressed him now rather than his mother.

Elena looked him straight in the eye as she spoke. "Another time, Jesus said, 'But when the Comforter is come, whom I will send unto you from the Father, even the Spirit of truth, which proceedeth from the Father, he shall testify of me: And ye also shall bear witness, because ye have been with me from the beginning.' "

"Jesus said that?" A frown tugged at the corners of his mouth. "That the Comforter would testify about Him?"

Elena nodded. "So how could the Comforter possibly be Mohammed? Mohammed does not testify about Jesus being God's Son and neither was Mohammed with Jesus when He spoke these words."

"No, of course not," Auhan agreed. "Mohammed didn't live until more than six hundred years after Jesus."

"That's right." Elena face brightened again at his response.

"It's all so amazing!" his mother exclaimed.

"Amazing and true—and the reason why I am able to turn my problems over to God, *Anne* Fatima," Elena said, returning to the original question. "He is not only my heavenly Father but my friend too."

Radiance seemed to fill his mother's face as she nodded. "I think I understand now. It's as if a veil," she moved her hands as if she were removing a cloth from her face, "has been taken away from my eyes, and for the first time I can see, can understand, that which I only sensed before."

She looked down at the cross in her hands. "God is a personal God who is not only above me as my heavenly Father," she paused, as though savoring a sweet, new wonder, "but He is with me in Jesus Christ and in me through the Comforter, the Holy Ghost." She turned to him.

"The Comforter whom Jesus talks about is another nature of God, Auhan. It's true!" She crossed her arms across her chest. "I feel it here."

He looked for a long moment at his mother. He was glad to see her so joyful, yet he still felt very unsure. He glanced over at his father but found no help there. The older man wore an enigmatic expression that gave nothing away.

Auhan turned to Elena. As expected, she wore the same radiant expression as his mother.

He wondered, could something that made others so happy be wrong? He didn't know. However, he did know he had ruined enough moments for his mother during the last year, and he resolved not to mar this one by voicing any more doubts or by leaving the cabin, as he had the last time the discussion had turned religious.

"What do I have to do?" Fatima asked Elena. She responded by touching a bandaged hand to his mother's arm.

"Scripture tells us, 'But as many as received him, to them gave he power to become the sons of God, even to them that believe on his name: Which were born, not of blood, nor of the will of the flesh, nor of the will of man, but of God.' "

The phrase "born. . .of God" jumped out at Auhan, but Elena didn't notice the look of wondering inquiry he sent her way. She continued her explanation of the recited scripture to his mother.

"*Anne*, to all who believe in the redemptive blood of Jesus

Christ, God gives them the right to be counted as sons and daughters. All you have to do is to repent of your sin—tell Him you're sorry. Confess your belief in Jesus Christ as His Son. Then, accept the gift of His salvation, which He bought for us with His atoning death."

"That's all?" There was an incredulous note in his mother's voice.

"That's it," Elena replied. "Believe me, *Anne* Fatima, afterwards you will find yourself really wanting to please God. But your salvation won't depend on what you do. Your salvation has already been bought by Jesus. All you have to do to please God, to be counted as God's daughter, is to believe Jesus, believe He spoke the truth when He said, 'I am the way, the truth, and the life: no man cometh unto the Father, but by me.' "

Auhan realized just how amazing such a concept must be to his mother. The idea seemed too incredible to him as well. Like his mother, he had been raised to believe that one must earn Allah's mercy and the rewards of heaven through good deeds. He could hardly grasp the idea that God, through Jesus, freely gave salvation to them who would simply repent and believe.

In answer to Elena, his mother's chest swelled on a deep, new breath, as though she breathed in a new air of freedom.

"Would you like me to pray with you?" Elena offered.

Fatima shook her head. "No. I wish to go and commune with my God alone." Casting a smile at each of them, she turned and walked out of the cabin.

As she left, Auhan's mind filled with questions concerning what had just happened to her. There was so much about this whole discussion that he didn't understand. He determined to ask Elena more questions.

But later.

Later.

seven

And having spoiled principalities and powers, he made a
shew of them openly, triumphing over them in it [the cross].
Colossians 2:15

The following days proved to be glorious ones. Not only did
God's light fill both *Anne* Fatima's heart and their little cabin,
but Elena's physical healing seemed to progress at a geometric
rate as well. Each day she witnessed a major improvement.
Her cough was breaking up, and her burns were healing.
Although her energy remained low, she rejoiced that she no
longer had to stay in bed. She could sit for several hours at a
time in an easy chair and sip her ever present cup of chamomile while enjoying the movement of the ship beneath her, the
wonderful ship that had not only rescued her but was carrying
her home to America.

One morning, her eyes spied a violin case tucked away in a
far corner of the cabin.

"Oh my," she exclaimed and looked toward Auhan. He sat
on his mother's bunk holding his hands apart and aloft as he
helped her turn a skein of yarn into a manageable ball. His
long and slender, aristocratic hands with their blunt nails
convinced Elena that he owned the instrument.

"Do you play the violin, Auhan?" She motioned toward
the case.

The guileless words no sooner left her mouth than Elena
knew she had stumbled onto a sensitive subject. *Anne* Fatima
paused her yarn rolling. Auhan's expression turned to stone.

Elena flicked her gaze toward Auhan's father. Like her, he seemed to be waiting for his son's answer.

"I used to," Auhan answered, tight-lipped and hard.

Elena looked at his hands. She studied them. She didn't see any scars, nor had she noticed him favoring his arms or hands in any way during the time she had been with them. Quite the contrary. Now that she thought about it, she had often noticed his fingers moving as if they fingered musical chords. She drew in a quick breath of amazement as the realization struck her. He had been doing just that. She had thought the strange movement just a nervous trait. She now knew otherwise.

He might not pick up and play the instrument, but the instrument often played him. She quickly surmised that his reason for not plucking and bowing on his violin must be of the mental, not physical, kind.

"I love the sound of the violin." She sensed that she, in blissful ignorance, might broach the subject of his musical abilities, even though he had strictly tabooed the issue for discussion by his parents.

From the moment she voiced her question, she had sensed a definite current of anticipation shooting back and forth between the couple. They appeared to wait with near breathless expectancy to see how their son would respond to her inquiry. Elena's own curiosity prodded her on as well, although Auhan obviously wished she would drop the matter.

She paused just long enough to measure her words. "My father often invited musicians into our home to give performances. String quartets were our favorites. One group in particular played the most wonderful rendition of Beethoven's 'Ode to Joy.' " She closed her eyes in remembrance and sighed. "Their music was sublime. We all loved it."

Opening her eyes again, she looked back at him. His jaw

muscles rippled to show his tension, and he purposefully avoided her gaze by scrutinizing some indefinable point near the ceiling of the cabin.

She offered him the most encouraging smile she could muster, despite his refusal to look at her. "I'll bet with those long fingers, you make sweet music."

"He makes the most wonderful sounds emerge from any instrument," Auhan's father spoke from his bunk, with the gravelly voice of a person unaccustomed to speaking. Elena looked at him in surprise. Although he often sent smiles and good feelings in her direction, the older man rarely uttered a word.

Nodding in appreciation of the information, Elena turned back to Auhan and ventured to say, "I'd love to hear you some—"

"I don't play anymore," he growled, slinging the skein of yarn onto the bunk. He grabbed his cap and stalked out of the room, not even motioning, as he normally did, for Buddy to follow him.

Elena stiffened. As she listened to his feet thump along the passageway, she decided Auhan dealt with all the topics that disturbed him by stomping away. She threw a disgusted look at the door through which he had, yet again, disappeared in a masculine huff. When she regained her strength, he wouldn't find it so easy to walk away from her. She regarded the empty doorway for a moment longer. Then, when she could no longer hear his hard footfall, she turned her eyes back to his parents. Her heart went out to them.

They sat apart and yet together in a world of parental misery. The defeated slouch of their shoulders, their vacant stares, their short, quick breaths—each evidenced their sadness and pain.

Not knowing quite what to do or what to say, Elena looked down at her ever present sidekick, Buddy. As if he picked up on the tension in the air, he let out a soft "hurumph" and rested his chin upon Elena's knee in that canine way meant to impart comfort. Elena placed her hand upon his head. Just rubbing the tips of her fingers in little circles upon his crown acted as a tranquilizer, one she wished she could offer to Fatima and Suleiman.

As much as Elena wanted to ask what the violin had to do with such a display of mood on Auhan's part, she didn't feel that she should pry. More than anything, she was beginning to get annoyed with Auhan's sulking temper. She liked him, sometimes more than she knew she should, but she was also perturbed with his thinking that he could continually hurt his parents in this way. Surely they weren't to blame for whatever had caused him to stop playing that curvaceous instrument.

Just when Elena decided nothing further would be said, Fatima's low, hurting voice drifted across the cabin's screaming silence in the wake of Auhan's departure.

"Our two sons are extremely gifted young men." Tears shimmered but did not fall from *Anne* Fatima's intense eyes.

"Auhan's soul sings through the instrument," she motioned over to the violin case, "as our eldest does through words." She paused, and the muscles of her face tightened, making her look years older than her reported age of forty-one.

"But Auhan was terribly traumatized last year by things that happened when he was with his army—things he hasn't even told us about in full." Her thin shoulders shuddered beneath her dark dress in the distressed movement of a mother who felt helpless. "Our other son. . .we don't even know for certain if he lives," she whispered. Opening her fingers, she dropped the ball of yarn onto the bunk, and tucking her elbows against her chest, she cradled her face in her hands.

Elena's heart broke for *Anne* Fatima. The poor woman didn't even know if her first-born son was alive, and every mile they traveled took her farther and farther away from their homeland.

Elena leaned toward the head of her bunk and wiggled her fingers under her pillow until she felt the cloth containing her mother's cross. Since she was now well enough to care for both it and the wedding ring set, *Anne* Fatima had returned the jewelry to her the previous day. With the cross in hand, she pushed the rings back under her pillow and slowly rose from her chair. She hadn't stood unassisted since her ordeal, and her knees shook as she took small, hesitant steps over to the older woman. Bracing herself against the wall, she held out the cross to Fatima.

"*Anne* Fatima, I want you to have this." Elena knew a new Christian needed a reminder of her faith—especially when dealing with something as difficult as having one of her children missing somewhere in the world.

Fatima regarded the cross for a long moment as it dangled from its gold chain in front of her eyes. Suddenly, she jumped to her feet.

"You shouldn't be walking on your own, dear girl—" She just managed to place her steadying grip beneath Elena's elbows as the boat rolled on a wave. In the same moment, Elena felt herself losing her balance, and she grabbed hold of Fatima's arms. "Especially in such rough seas." Waves crashed against the hull of the ship to punctuate the older woman's admonishment.

Elena gave a nervous, self-conscious laugh. She couldn't believe how weak she still felt. "I'll sit." When she did, she immediately held the cross out to Fatima once again, not wanting to forget her original purpose in approaching the other woman. "Please," she fought to stay the cough that rose within her from the exertion of her small walk, "accept this, dear friend. Please."

Fatima looked from Elena to the cross and back again. She made a negative gesture with her hand. "No, I can't. It's too valuable." Elena knew Fatima was well acquainted with expensive jewelry. She had told Elena how her jewelry—the selling of much of it, the careful protection of the rest—had enabled her family to make this move.

"It is valuable." Elena didn't try to deny its worth. "But mostly because of the meaning behind it and because it belonged to my mother. But I know she would be very pleased for you to have it." She coughed a little, but she refused to let a coughing fit swallow the words that needed to be said. "You have not only been God's instrument toward saving my life, but you now understand the meaning behind the cross and believe the truth for which it stands." Her throat muscles worked as she tried to suppress yet another cough.

While Fatima handed Elena her cup of tea, a small smile creased the older woman's lips. "Like my ancestors long before me, I now know."

Her newfound knowledge and faith seemed to give *Anne* a great deal of satisfaction—as if a cycle had somehow successfully been completed.

After a few sips of the warm liquid, Elena had her coughing reflexes under control again. She placed the cup on the bedside chest and reached out to take *Anne's* work-worn hands within her own. She nestled the cross in her palms.

"The cross of Jesus is yours, my dear friend in Christ. You understand its meaning—its redemptive meaning—probably better than most. Please take this symbol of that most glorious event in history and, whenever doubts about either of your sons invade your mind, look at it and keep faith. God will look after your sons."

Fatima's eyes clung to the cross now cradled lovingly within the palm of her hand. "More than anything I'm afraid that it might be too late and that they may not find the faith of their long-ago ancestors."

Elena knew that she was voicing her deepest fear. She shook her head. "It is never too late. Let's just keep praying."

Looking over at her ever silent husband, Fatima appeared on the verge of tears. The two gazed at one another with a love that had weathered many storms in life. Elena could tell Fatima would not have changed him for all the men in the world—despite his quiet nature. He gave his wife a short nod of his gray head, encouraging his wife to accept the cross. Fatima looked back at Elena and relayed the nod. "Dear Daughter, I would be honored to accept your mother's cross and the reminder it stands for. Thank you."

❧

Elena fell asleep praying for the brooding young man, Auhan. The last prayerful thought she remembered before she drifted off to sleep had been a request that he might once again take his violin in his beautiful hands and draw melody from the instrument.

A musician!

Elena had no musical talent of her own, but she loved listening to music. Like most who could neither carry a note in song nor play a tune, she had a great respect and appreciation for those who could.

Her father had always told her that people with such passions—writing, teaching, playing an instrument, painting, drawing, doctoring, creating stained glass windows, figuring scientific calculations—any creative thing, if they didn't do what they had been fashioned to do, they could never be totally content. Talent came with a price—the price of obedience to use what God had given them. And when a person didn't use their talent, the fear that their talent would be taken away haunted them, tormented them.

Auhan returned later in the afternoon just as Elena awakened from her second nap of the day. Although no one mentioned the earlier episode, she had learned a great deal about Auhan as a result of his behavior. She now knew part of his problem stemmed from his no longer playing the violin as well as what had happened to him the previous year. Elena believed these two things, combined with his doubts about the Almighty, held him in the grip of lonely and confused misery. With a degree of certainty, Elena thought he owed his alienation to a deep sense of guilt.

She had often read guilt in his expressive eyes. The encompassing emotion enveloped him like a dark cloud and turned him into a sullen young man. Of course, she had no idea why he felt guilty. She doubted if even his parents knew why. But her father had taught her the real issue had little to do with why a person feels guilty. Ridding them of the debilitating emotion was the important thing. Guilt ate away at a person like a cancer. God never intended people to contend with their guilt by themselves.

Elena's young heart went out to Auhan. She knew all sin and its resulting guilt could be assuaged only by the power of the risen Lord, the Lord Jesus Christ. She wanted the free gift of salvation, deliverance from all his sins, to be Auhan's. In spite of his moods, he was becoming more and more dear to her. Although he was one of the most handsome young men she had ever met, her reasons went deeper than such a superficial attraction. She had often caught a look in his eyes, a flicker—as if his soul held a wick just waiting to be quickened. She hoped to be on hand when the spark burst into flame. She could just imagine how bright his deep-set brown eyes would shine.

eight

*Humble yourselves therefore under the mighty hand of
God, that he may exalt you in due time: Casting all your care
upon him; for he careth for you.*
1 Peter 5:6–7

Days sailed one upon another.

Although the ocean had been blowing a tempest for nearly
half a week and the little ship rocked and rolled in the heavy
sea, Auhan was amazed by how it didn't bother the ladies in
his cabin in the least. He had overheard fellow passengers
speaking, and he knew the few other female passengers aboard
the *Ionian Star* were suffering greatly.

He marveled even more at Elena. With her regained health,
the recollection of what she had gone through and lost came
into sharper focus. Yet, although she mourned the loss of her
father and often talked about her sister and little Rose, the
light shining from Elena's soul seemed to shine brighter and
brighter as her body became stronger and stronger.

The change in his mother equally astounded him. With all
the love of a child for his parent, Auhan had always wished
such an all-encompassing happiness for her. Yet even when
he had played the violin expressly for her, she hadn't looked
as joyful as she did now.

Almost, but not quite.

Auhan recognized his mother was not only happy, she was
at peace. He had made her glad when he played his violin.
Proud too in that manner in which parents specialize and

upon which children thrive. But, ever since his mother had made the decision to return to the religion of her ancestors, the inner tranquillity, which had always eluded her before, now radiated from her. He hadn't even realized this serenity—this peace, which seemed different from anything a mere mortal could give to another—had been the missing quality. She seemed lighter somehow. Freer. No longer carrying heavy emotional burdens on her slender shoulders. Her every step reflected this new freedom. She bounced everywhere she went.

He had noticed the cross hanging around her neck, but he withheld any comment. Although he was still very suspect of spiritual matters, he knew he liked the way his mother's new belief had helped her. The realization softened his heart a little toward the Christian God. Finally, the God of Jesus Christ seemed to be helping someone.

The light shining from his mother's eyes, which used to be so dull in comparison, gave him a moment's pause each time she held his gaze. Her eyes were almost as bright and radiant as Elena's.

Almost.

Not quite.

Yet, Auhan felt certain that with time, they might blaze just as brightly. Somehow.

ଈ

They had been in the Atlantic for several days when their little ship sailed into a perfect calm. After days of rough seas, it was a pleasant change, even to those unaffected by the motion of a ship. For Suleiman, who didn't possess a stomach in tune with sea travel, the reprieve brought back into the older man's cheeks a color that had been missing.

The sun shone brightly into the cabin, and to Elena, it felt more like a midsummer's day than one of the first days of autumn. As more of a summer person than a winter one, she savored the feeling.

An unexpected knock on the wall to the side of the opened cabin door brought her attention to a distinguished-looking man wearing a blue uniform replete with a double row of shiny brass buttons traveling down its front.

"So, how's our 'Dolphin Girl' today?" The man's words possessed the clipped sounds of a decidedly New England accent. Regarding him, Elena felt certain she had to be looking at the captain of the *Ionian Star*.

Of medium height, but with a sturdiness of body brought on by life aboard a ship, the mariner looked as if a traveling drama company had cast him to play the captain's role in a production. From his white-trimmed whiskers and his ruddy complexion to his twinkling but ever observant eyes, he epitomized Elena's idea of how an American sea captain should look. At first sight, Elena liked him.

"Captain," Auhan exclaimed in English. His tone held more excitement than Elena thought he was capable of showing. He immediately stood and offered the distinguished man his seat. Auhan obviously held a great respect for the man.

"A nice. . .surprise. . .this. . .is," Fatima spoke in halting but gracious English. She rose from her bunk and went to stand before the captain. "A tea. . .you would. . .like? Yes?"

"That would be lovely, Madam," he responded with equal grace. Then, he trained his sharp yet kind eyes on Elena. "Dear 'Dolphin Girl,' I am so glad to see you looking so well. I must say, you gave all onboard this vessel, myself included, quite a scare."

Elena rolled her eyes and nodded. "I gave myself quite a scare too." She smiled as the older man chuckled. The sound reminded Elena of her father. She rejoiced in hearing the laugh.

"But what do you mean by 'Dolphin Girl'?"

"Don't you know? That's what you are called by all on-board this ship." He looked around the cabin at the others. "You didn't tell her about how she was saved?"

Elena didn't even give Fatima, whose mouth was poised to answer, the time to respond.

"Oh, I remember, Captain," Elena assured him. "The moonlight dance of the dolphins jumping and leaping all around me in the sea is not something I shall ever forget. I just didn't realize all the other passengers were aware of my unusual rescue."

He answered with a respectful bow of his head. "I have heard my fair share of dolphin stories in my more than fifty years at sea, but never have I actually witnessed such a rescue in action." He shook his head and reached over to pat Buddy. "Auhan told me about how the dolphin had first saved this dog, brought him to you, then saved you both." He shook his head again. "What an amazing God we have," he proclaimed.

Elena's eyes opened wide, even as her spirit made an excited leap within her. Regarding him with a new, specific interest, she felt compelled to ask, "Are you. . .a. . .believer, Captain?"

"Most definitely," he answered without hesitation. Smiling his thanks to Fatima, he took the cup of tea that she held out to him. "That is one of the reasons I try to travel in the Levant as much as I possibly can," he continued to Elena. "I not only like sailing those historic waters, but often I try to take excursions in which I might visit the sights of early Christianity. The Near East—Asia Minor—has always been one of my favorite places."

A pleased smile curved Elena's lips. Now she understood there was a lot more to this captain than just his seafaring abilities. "That's wonderful, Captain. Since you have the opportunity, how marvelous it is for your Christian walk that you take it."

The captain nodded in agreement while he placed his teacup and saucer on the table. "It has helped immensely. I firmly believe if not for the rational minds of those early Greeks when the apostles walked Asia Minor's beautiful land, Christianity would never have reached the northern shores of my ancestors in far-off Britain—and most other nations of people, for that matter, even the distant, then-future shores of America. For that, all of Christendom should forever be grateful."

Elena's brows came together in a quick frown. "The Christians of the world certainly didn't act too grateful while they sat safely on their ships in Smyrna's harbor and watched the destruction of one of Christendom's oldest cities," she shot back before realizing how bitter she sounded. Color flooded her face. "Forgive me," she whispered and looked down.

"So," the captain said. The word spoke volumes. "That is what happened in Smyrna. Many conflicting press reports have come over the wireless. One hardly knows what to believe." He raised his hands in a show of helplessness before letting them fall back onto his knees. "But I had suspected as much."

His words reminded Elena of something her father had told her during their trip to Washington the previous May. "My father believed that if the Greco-Turkish War should end with the defeat of the Greeks, before this century passes, few people will realize Asia Minor was predominantly a Greek land—and a Christian one—much, much longer than it has politically been a land of the Turks."

"I believe your father to be correct," the captain replied.

Elena continued, feeling free to talk to her countryman about these issues she had longed to voice for days. "Near the beginning of recorded history—nearly three thousand years ago—Smyrna was peacefully settled by Greeks who offered a better way of life, a civilized life. A life that appealed to all who experienced it. Their culture and civilization—the polis, city—made Asia Minor one of the most advanced places on earth for much more than twenty-five hundred years."

The city of her father's ancestors was now gone, and Elena ached with the knowledge. "Even after Asia Minor's occupation by the Ottoman Turks—who used Greek know-how to build their empire—it was the Christians of the land who were the backbone of the economy. Up until last week." She shrugged her shoulders slightly. "That's how it always was."

"As a transporter of cargo I am very aware of all of this," the captain concurred. "One has only to walk through Asia Minor and see the graceful ruins of a civilization, both ancient and medieval, to realize their beauty surpasses much of what is to be found in our modern world, my dear." The captain obviously wanted to impart comfort. "If a person doesn't have such an opportunity, one need only pick up a Bible and read the letters penned to the Greek cities or study church history for a powerful reminder."

Elena dipped her head. "But I don't think many will do as you suggest," she reflected. "My father also told me people are too lazy to learn the truth. And even if they want to learn, press reports today cannot be trusted. Soon, even history books will be changed to reflect the angle the governments find most beneficial. They cater only to the god of commerce—the god they are coming to worship more and more in this twentieth century."

The captain's eyebrows rose in obvious surprise at her knowledge of political matters.

"You are a very bright young lady," the captain responded after a moment.

Elena offered him a self-conscious smile. "My father wanted my sister and me to be aware of what was going on around us." A look of sadness crossed her face. "Actually, in spite of his teachings, we were, until last week, very naïve."

She remembered how her father had wanted them to remain in Washington the previous May until the Greco-Turkish War was resolved. They had insisted on returning with him to Smyrna rather than face separation from their much-loved and respected father. Neither Elena nor Sophia ever imagined Smyrna, in these modern days, could be pillaged and utterly destroyed.

"Any wisdom you see in me now, Captain," she continued after a moment, "has come from the bitter pill of experience. I've witnessed things people should never have to see."

The captain's lips pursed together beneath his mustache. "Oftentimes experience is the best teacher, my dear, albeit the hardest."

"Captain, do you know about all the Christians who were killed under cover of the Great War by the Turkish government?" Again her words left her mouth before she took time to consider them.

&

She was asking the captain, but Auhan's heart nearly skipped a beat at her mention of this occurrence, a small portion of which he had stumbled upon the previous year. He hadn't realized she knew about the executions, his country's so-called "deportations" of Christians. Knowing about them, how could she be so open to him, a former Turkish soldier?

As if he were watching one of those new moving pictures he had heard about, he watched as the captain again nodded his head, this time with a seriousness of movement Auhan was sure he normally reserved for matters pertaining to the safe running of his ship.

"In 1917 our president, Woodrow Wilson, wanted to declare war on the Turks because they were strong allies of the Germans. But the lobbying of American missionaries prevented his doing so for the ostensible reason that a declaration of war would have meant abandoning the millions of Christians—Greeks, Armenian, American missionaries, and others—living there."

Auhan was amazed as he watched Elena dip her head in knowledgeable concurrence to this tidbit of recent history. He had no idea the then-president of the United States had desired to declare war upon the Turks.

"Ironically, if the missionaries hadn't lobbied against the declaration, things would have probably been much better for the Christians of the Near East," the captain commented. "For most regrettably and sadly," he continued with a gravity of expression, "what followed was the worst mass extermination of people our modern time has ever seen. The Armenians and the Greeks have suffered terrible things under Turkish rule." He glanced Auhan's way, as if he dared him to refute it. But Auhan wouldn't. He knew better than most the truth found in the captain's words.

ba

"So tell me, Captain," Elena persisted. She could feel Auhan watching her, but she averted her gaze and studied the epaulets on the captain's coat. "Why did the Christians allow it to happen again, just last week? Why did all those allied ships filled with men representing Christians from England, France, America, Italy—friendly nations, allies of Greece—just sit in the harbor and watch thousands more brethren die?"

The captain pursed his lips, and Elena waited for his response as he weighed his words.

"I don't really think most of the men onboard the ships really knew what was going on."

Elena nodded her head in agreement. "You are correct, of course, Captain," she replied. "I remember many of the sailors had stricken looks upon their faces."

"And those few who did, well. . ." The captain opened his hands before him. "My dear, just because a person labels himself a Christian doesn't necessarily mean that he is. . . actually. . .a. . .Christian. And further, how many people in positions of authority are true believers—people who have a deep and personal relationship with God, as revealed by Jesus, the Christ? I personally doubt many politicians—presidents, prime ministers, generals, kings, queens—are truly Christians. Otherwise, we wouldn't have all these terrible wars. I believe most in positions of authority—most, but not all," he qualified, "are more concerned about commerce and the accumulation of wealth for themselves and their nation. The Christians of Smyrna got in the way of those who worship that god you mentioned a few moments ago, the god of commerce."

She dipped her head. "But, please forgive me. You have come for a friendly visit—I don't know what made me speak of such things." Remorse filled her words. She feared she showed a total lack of the social graces. If Sophia had been here, she would have received a thorough scolding upon the captain's departure.

But the captain showed no sign of being offended. With a kind, sad smile, he offered, "Seeing your city destroyed is motive enough for such talk, my dear."

Elena looked up at the captain and, taking a deep breath, whispered, "It used to be so pretty."

"I know. I've gone into Smyrna many times when picking up cargo. It was one of the prettiest cities in the Levant."

Elena nodded in agreement. In her mind's eye, she saw again her final glimpse of Smyrna that last horrible night she swam next to the rowboat toward the rescue ship. The city had groaned, lamented, as flames licked upward, trapping thousands of people in an area a mile and a half long by one hundred feet wide. And the desperate, frantic wails of the people filled her head.

"Elena," she heard Fatima call out to her and realized that her breathing had become fast and hard. She blinked and forced herself to slowly draw in large, controlling breaths of air.

"I'm sorry," she murmured and gave Fatima a reassuring smile. "Sometimes, when I remember back to Smyrna burning, . . ." She gave a slight shudder. She couldn't go on.

With the gentle comfort of a grandfather, the captain gave her arm a soft pat and rose from his chair. "When you are stronger, we shall talk more. To talk is something good. But it is infinitely better to give to God those thoughts that are too hard or too heavy for you to carry." Elena's gaze flicked over to Fatima's.

The older woman smiled at Elena and then turned to the captain to explain their reaction. "That. . .she do, yes. Give problems. . .to God. I do too, that."

The captain regarded Fatima with a look of wonder. "You are a believer, Madam?"

Fatima glanced down at Elena, and they exchanged another of the special mother-daughter smiles they had become accustomed to sharing over the last few days. This little interchange communicated more than a thousand words ever could.

Fatima turned back to the captain and answered him. "When I come to ship." She paused. Crinkling her eyelids together in concentration, she corrected herself. "When I came on ship. No, I was not. But now. Yes."

"I wish I had known," the captain returned. "You could have come to Sunday service yesterday."

"You have church?" Fatima asked, puzzlement drawing lines on her face.

"I hold a service each Sunday. To pastor those of my crew and passengers who are Christians is my very favorite duty as captain. I would be very pleased for you all to come to service on the next Lord's Day, Kyriakie," he qualified, using the Greek word and meaning for the day of worship.

"Only my mother and Elena are Christians," Auhan interjected.

The captain regarded him with a steady, measuring gaze. "You would still be welcomed, Son. Since next Sunday is the last Sunday before arriving in New York, we are planning an extra special service too. One of my sailors, who is pretty handy with the fiddle in a folksy kind of way, has agreed to play."

A charge like a lightning bolt passed between Elena and Auhan, but she tore her gaze away from Auhan as the captain continued to speak. From the way the captain's blue eyes narrowed, Elena knew he had noticed the tension electrifying the air.

"The sailor doesn't like performing in formal settings. He enjoys the foot-stomping fiddle playing below deck much more. Nonetheless, we have a standing agreement that he will play for my church service the last Sunday before arriving in port."

"When do we arrive, Captain?" Elena asked and glanced back at Auhan. She was saddened to see a deep, brooding look settling in his eyes once again.

"God willing, early next week. We'll talk more, young lady." He walked toward the doorway and then turned back to them. "Goodness, I almost forgot the reason I came by—other than to meet the 'Dolphin Girl.' " His eyes held a twinkle as he looked down at her. "I wanted to suggest that you come and sit up on deck. We should be having several days of smooth sailing. Why don't you let the healing rays of the sun touch you?"

"Oh." Elena's eyes widened, and she was both amazed and very happy to realize the idea appealed to her. She must truly be getting better. Until that day she had felt no desire to be out in the elements. But with joy filling her, she realized the thought of the sun's rays touching on her skin didn't bother her at all anymore. "I'd like that, Captain, very much. Thank you."

He nodded his head, then frowned. "You don't have a fever any longer, do you?"

Elena laughed. "The only fever I have now is cabin fever."

"Good." He sent her his ready smile. "That is a fever I can help cure. I'll have a sailor set up a canopy on the upper deck and place a chair there for you." He glanced down at her bandaged hands. "You don't want to let your burns feel the sun yet."

She slightly dipped her head in agreement. "Thank you, Captain."

"Don't mention it, my 'Dolphin Girl.' " His eyes filled with merriment as he smiled down on her. He turned to Auhan. "Shall I have one of my sailors carry her up on deck or will you be able to manage it?"

"It will be my honor, Sir. Besides," Auhan glanced down at Elena and shocked her—thrilled her—by winking, "this 'Dolphin Girl' and I have a long-standing date to sit deckside."

As the captain looked from one to the other, Elena felt heat rising in her cheeks, and she knew they were turning red. He gave a hearty chuckle, which reminded Elena so much of her dear father.

"Now why doesn't that surprise me?" Placing his hat upon his head, he touched its brim. "Until later." He turned and walked briskly up the passageway away from them.

Elena looked up at Auhan.

He looked down at her.

He smiled.

She, of course, smiled back.

nine

In him was life;
and the life was the light of men.
And the light shineth in darkness;
and the darkness comprehended it not.
John 1:4–5

Two hours later, Auhan ambled over to where Elena sat, waiting, on her chair. Fatima and Suleiman had just left the cabin to retrieve cleaning supplies. They planned on cleaning the room from top to bottom while Elena was out.

"Don't you look nice," he commented. Looking up at him, Elena noticed a special sparkle in the depth of his dark, chestnut eyes—a sparkle she had never noticed before.

Blushing slightly, Elena tore her gaze away from the unfamiliar but very welcomed glint. She glanced down at the soft china blue dress she wore for her reintroduction to the outside world. Of plain cotton, it was probably the least expensive dress to have ever touched her skin. Yet, because the garment had belonged to Fatima, who had stayed up late several nights altering it to fit Elena's smaller frame, it was also her most beloved one.

Elena completed her outfit by draping a white, lightweight shawl around her back, and then she turned back to Auhan. "Promise you won't drop me?" she bantered, wanting to hide the nervous thrill she felt at the idea of Auhan carrying her.

She hadn't considered this part of their "date" the first time he mentioned their sitting together on deck. But she had been able to think of little else since Auhan had declared to the captain his intentions to transport her outside. Elena was finally beginning to understand how her sister felt about Christos. The idea of being so close to Auhan, as near as his carrying her would bring them, did unexpected but very pleasant things to her heart.

What had started out as prayers for Auhan were now day-long thoughts of him. Elena couldn't seem to stop thinking of him. She wasn't quite sure when her unceasing prayers for him had turned into her constantly dreaming of a life together with him.

"I wouldn't drop you anymore than I would the most precious crystal in the world." Warm amusement flavored his voice. His words made Elena's nerves quiver all the way to her toes.

Reaching down, he placed one arm beneath her legs, which the long length of the dress concealed in a decorous way. His other went across her shoulders.

The ease with which he lifted her from the chair surprised her. Christos had carried Sophia when she fainted by the side of their home after having been attacked, but Christos was a huge man. Auhan wasn't much taller than Elena and of slight build. Feeling the rippling motion of his muscles beneath his jacket, she learned how his strength had been deceptively hidden by his size. For a moment, he just held her against him, as if gauging her weight.

"As I thought, you're lightweight," he commented, and she could hear the smile in his voice.

Not quite knowing where to rest her gaze, she looked down at her fingers as they lay upon her chest. Excitement and wonder at being so near to him sent funny little tremors through her body. He smelled of rope hemp and ocean breeze, a heady, masculine scent that left her weak and slightly woozy. Being this close to him made her aware of him in an adult way, a way in which she had never felt before.

His breath brushed warm against her neck when he spoke again. "But, if you could just place your left arm around my shoulders, it would be even easier for me." Mirth deepened his voice still further.

"Oh." She felt heat rush to her face as she quickly did as he requested. Her color intensified when he chuckled. A gloriously male sound rumbled out from his chest.

"Elena," he said as he left the cabin, the dog at his heals. "You are adorable. We have been sleeping in the same room ever since you came aboard, and for the first time since we've met, you are properly dressed." He glanced down at her dainty feet. His mother had even found a pair of ankle-strap pumps for her. "And yet, you are embarrassed."

"It is because I am dressed," she countered, but seeing his brows rise in a manly way of question, she huffed out a breath and quickly continued to explain that which she felt was obvious. "What I mean is, for the first time, I am not a sick patient."

"Ah. . ." He nodded his head, and she was conscious of a subtle glint in his eyes as he suggested dryly, "You mean, you are a woman?"

She looked at him squarely in the face. She had seen how he had looked at her when he thought she hadn't been noticing. She had very good peripheral vision, and she knew that he "liked" her every bit as much as she "liked" him.

"Aren't I? A woman, I mean?" she asked in direct challenge.

～ ❧

With her face just a scant two inches from his own, he wondered if she had any idea about the inner turmoil she stirred to life within him. He suspected she was too young and too inexperienced to really understand what a woman could do to a man. These two qualities about her didn't bother him in the least.

But to address her question. Was she a woman? Most definitely. His own body pressed, as it was, against her own made him all too painfully aware of this fact. Actually, she was a woman who felt wonderful in his arms. Even more, one to whom he didn't want to say good-bye when their ship arrived in New York City in a few days.

"You are," he finally answered, not able to control the deep huskiness in his voice any more than he could still his wildly beating heart. "A very beautiful one, at that."

Her lips parted and curved in a spontaneous, timid response, and Auhan felt as if all the flowers of spring were contained within her smile.

"Thank you, Auhan." She reached up with her right hand and gently touched around the burned area on her left cheek as well as the one at the hairline on her forehead. "It's nice to hear," she shrugged her shoulders slightly, "—after all this."

"Ah. . .Elena." He shook his head, quickly denying that she had any reason to worry. "Those scars might fade away." He looked directly at the burn on her cheek—the worst one— and paused to study it. Almost the size of an American silver dollar, it was red and sore looking. The pain it had caused her—still gave her—ate away at him. But swallowing his anger, refusing to let it divert his thoughts or mar their outing, he continued, "But if the scars never disappear, you are beautiful. You don't need to depend on physical appearance to be beautiful," he qualified. "That light which shines out from your soul is so bright, it's all a person sees when they meet you."

Her eyes widened as though surprised to hear him being so complimentary. Perhaps she simply enjoyed hearing his words of true compliment. "What a nice thing to say, Auhan.

Thank you." She paused, and Auhan watched as she kneaded her lower lip with her teeth.

"I pray. . ." She hesitated and, with a look of uncertainty, searched his face before she ventured to speak her mind. "I pray, that it is. . .a light. . .which you will someday come to have."

He dropped his smile, but he continued to search her face for answers. In truth, Auhan longed to possess such a light within his own soul. He sensed the light illuminating Elena's soul came from an unlimited source. He almost wished Elena, as the friend she had become, could just give him a share of her inner light. But he also knew such a dream was senseless, as nonsensical as his wish to be reborn. To be handed such a gift, free and clear, would be too easy, and in this evil world in which they lived, it was not to be expected.

Not wanting to say or do anything that might ruin this day, he murmured, "I hope you are right." Even as he spoke the words, he was surprised to realize how much he really meant them. He would like to have the light she possessed—the light his mother now seemed to enjoy as well. But in order to be a bearer of such light, he sensed he would first need a soul free of guilt and anger. But he didn't expect such a thing could ever happen.

Not to him.

Not after the horrors he had seen. Not without a fresh start. A whole new life. And people just weren't given a second chance, even if they moved, as he was doing, to a land far, far away. The emotions forged by the former life would still be with a person. Hanging onto him. Pulling him down.

He came upon the doorway to the deck and twisted around so as not to bump either Elena's legs or her head against its hard edges. He stepped out into the sharp clearness of the sparkling day. Elena's laughter, a bubbly and light, infectious sound, filled the air and brought a quick and genuine smile to Auhan's lips as his attention returned to Elena and, thankfully, away from the contemplations of his mind.

"Oh, Auhan." She motioned out to the glorious day. "Look how beautiful the world is. So lovely," she sighed. "The clouds, the sky, the sea." She craned her neck and looked down into the placid water. "If only it had been this calm when I had been adrift in it." Auhan heard a wistful note to her voice. "I know things could have been many times worse," she hastened to qualify. "But this—it's like looking at a mirror of the sky."

Laughter, like water gurgling from a mountain spring, bubbled out of her again. Being near the edge of the ship didn't seem to bother her, so Auhan walked closer to the side. "Even the ship is almost perfectly reflected in it." She pointed down to the image of the *Ionian Star* portrayed in the peaceful, green sea through which it glided.

Auhan understood what she meant. A most remarkable day, it was as if the ship moved across a placid summer lake and not one of the vastest bodies of water on earth. But more than the ocean, it was the woman in his arms whom Auhan wanted to watch.

Like a baby being introduced to the world, she looked all around her until she settled her gaze on the horizon and the fluffy white clouds drifting above it. He could tell she was using all her senses, not just sight, to experience this moment. Tilting her head slightly to the side, she appeared to be both listening to the ship-generated breeze as well as feeling it upon her skin. From the way her chest rose and fell with a few deep breaths, he was certain she was sniffing the ocean-scented air. By the way her mouth slightly parted, he had no doubt she tasted the saltiness of the sea upon her red lips.

Her red lips. . .

He watched them as she moved the tip of her tongue across their smooth contour. With a start, he noticed the cuts and blisters, which had been a part of them ever since he had met her, had all but disappeared somewhere between yesterday and today. Yesterday, her mouth had still possessed a bit of puffy redness around its rims. Today, her lips looked smooth and so perfect, so appealing. He wanted nothing more than to lower his own lips to them, to taste them, to feel them, to—

The direction of his thoughts drew him up sharp. He pulled his eyes away from her face and to the horizon upon which she still gazed. He hadn't noticed a woman in so long that the feelings growing within him for Elena had gone unrecognized. Until now.

Now, all was different—and much more complicated. With Elena he felt much more than just a desire to kiss. He wished for a life together with her, a chance to see her smile every single day of his existence.

Turning abruptly away from both the railing and his thoughts, Auhan nearly swiped a sailor across his weathered face with Elena's pointy shoes. He instinctively drew back, even as the sailor ducked. Although the sailor had been trained to guard against dangerous parts of the ship or cargo that had worked its way loose, he was obviously surprised by having to maneuver in order to avoid the sharp tips of a woman's shoes.

"Hey, Mate," he called out. A wide, toothless grin split his face.

"I apologize." Auhan rushed to take the blame while Elena placed her hand over her mouth. She bent her knees back trying to lower the offending shoes. "I'm sorry too."

"No reason for either of ya to feel sorry, Ma'am," the sailor was quick to assure her. "Me and me mates," he motioned to the three sailors who hovered behind him, twirling their hats, "just wanted to see how ya was doing. We was the ones who spied ya among all them jumpin' dolphins and pulled ya from the sea th' other night," he declared, his chest puffing out with pride.

"Oh," Elena gasped and landed a smile upon each of the other men who stood looking on like embarrassed school-boys. Elena's heart went out to them, as did her free hand. In turn, she took each of their hands in her own, not caring when they motioned to their hands, soiled from work. She hadn't minded their dirty hands the night they had pulled her from the sea. She certainly didn't mind them now.

Then she spoke to each individually—to the spokesman first. "Thank you." They were two very common, often uttered words. Yet, she hoped the emotion she put into them left no doubt about the depth of her gratitude.

"Me pleasure, Ma'am," he responded, beaming as proudly as a new father might.

She turned to the next man. He had the softest blue eyes she had ever seen, even lighter in color than Sophia's.

"Thank you," she repeated to him her heartfelt appreciation.

"Me pleasure too, Ma'am. I am just glad to see ya so well." He blushed beet red when his mate jabbed at him, but he deflected the jab with expert agility. Elena smiled at their antics and turned to the one with curly brown hair and matching whiskers who had poked the second man.

"Thank you too, Sailor." She matched her tone to his out-going personality.

Sweeping his cap before him, he gave a little bow. "Just try and stay closer to shore when you go for a swim in the future, Missy." A bright smile accompanied his admonishment, and Elena knew for certain that she was addressing the jokester of the group. Her father had told her there was always one on every ship. Normally of above-average intelligence, the crew's jokester made life aboard a seagoing vessel "interesting" for everyone else.

"I will, indeed," she assured him and turned to the youngest man in the group. With hardly any whiskers on his face, he could not have been any older than she. Rather, she guessed him to be a couple of years younger.

"Thank you," she repeated the words but tried not to lose even a bit of their meaning as she reached for his hand and gave it a gentle squeeze. She'd thought the second sailor had been embarrassed, but this one couldn't even look her in the face. Lighting his gaze anywhere but at her, he plopped his hat back onto his head in order to be able to touch its brim in response.

"Hey, Boy." The jokester pulled the young sailor's cap off when he left it there. "Don't you know it's impolite to wear a hat in the presence of a lady?"

The boy looked as if he wished the sea would swallow him up, and Elena, always a bit of a joker herself, had a hard time containing the laughter threatening to bubble out from her. She was grateful when the toothless spokesman spoke up.

"We just wanted to make sure for ourselves that the 'Dolphin Girl' was as fine as the captain said." Elena caught Auhan's mirth-filled glance at the sailor's use of her new title.

She looked back at the sailor as he motioned to his buddies with his cap. "We all are happy to see you're fine."

"Thanks to you men and the dolphins," she murmured. "I'll never forget your finding me." Her face turned very serious. "I'm going to leave my name and the address with the captain so you may reach me. If any of you should ever need anything in the future—next month, next year, in ten years, or more," her gaze again lit upon each of the men, "please let me know. I would like to be able to help you or your families in the same measure you have helped me."

"Naw," the spokesman offered in quick response. "We don't want nothin'. Besides, the dolphins are the ones what saved ya. We never would've seen ya if they hadn't started jumpin' and movin' around like a bunch of bunnies in a forest."

Elena smiled at his analogy and thought, perhaps, he missed seeing trees and land creatures after having been at sea for so long. "Regardless, if ever I can be of assistance in any way, please let me know. I would not be here today if it hadn't been for your quick action. My father—" She paused and remembered back to the many times her father had assisted people. Of all his wealth, all his works of art, his assets, her father had never lost track of the fact that people were his greatest treasures—both close friends and strangers on the street. Her father had believed very strongly that God had so blessed him with wealth in order that he might prove himself a worthy steward and use his monetary means to help others. Elena would not forget his lesson or example. She lightly licked her lips and continued, "My father would want me to do so."

The sailors stuffed their hats back onto their heads and touched their brims to her in a show of respect. Then, Auhan returned their salutation with a nod of his own head and proceeded to carry her to the upper deck with Buddy close at his heels.

ten

Help those women which laboured with me
in the gospel. . .whose names are in the book of life.
Philippians 4:3

The canopy tented an easy chair in the shadiest part of the deck. The captain had thought of everything for her. Within easy reach, a small table held a teapot and several cups, all decorated with an interesting botanical design. A crate had been set in front of her chair so she could rest her legs.

Auhan lowered her to her feet with tender care.

Elena stood for a moment and enjoyed the vibration of the moving ship beneath the soles of her leather shoes. Then she turned a happy face toward Auhan.

"It's so wonderful to be outside again," she sighed. Not wanting to tax her strength, she sank into the chair and placed her legs upon the crate, taking care to arrange her skirt neatly and modestly around her legs.

Auhan lowered himself to the café-style chair provided for him, and they sat in companionable silence for several minutes while the surrounding sea played out its ancient tune.

The fresh, ocean-scented air wafted on the gentle breeze while the sounds of the sailors and the hum of the engines from deep within the bowels of the vessel provided welcome background sounds. Elena savored the moment. Being out on deck with Auhan proved to be even more wonderful than she had anticipated.

She treasured the ability to sit comfortably with someone

in silence. To communicate by talking might be necessary, but to communicate by just *being*—what a rare gift! Silent music filled the moment with a profound harmony—one that she suspected Auhan had been unable to capture and enjoy in a very long time.

"Thank you for bringing me out," Elena murmured after a few minutes. She turned her face to his and let out a peal of bubbly laughter. "And for holding me while I talked to the sailors." She nodded toward his back. "It must be hurting you."

"Not at all." He flashed her a smile. "Didn't I tell you that you were a lightweight?" He studied her with such intensity that his perusal sent a heat of embarrassment rushing to her cheeks.

She smiled but chose to bring the subject back to the sailors. "What a nice group of men. I thank God for them."

Auhan nodded. "I must say, they were sharp. When they realized you were in the middle of the jumping dolphins, they didn't waste even a second in getting you aboard. I overheard one of them say if they didn't move fast, they would lose you." He pointed to a lantern hanging on a peg just a short distance from them. "When they shone the lantern upon the sea and saw you, the stern of the ship had practically passed you by."

"I didn't know." She looked out at the huge expanse. From the safety of the ship's deck, the sea seemed so friendly. Yet, she knew how fast the raw elements could wear down a human or a land animal should one be tossed into the ocean's depths. She glanced down at her much-loved Buddy.

"Do you think, after what has happened, you will ever want to swim again?" Auhan ventured to ask. "You were literally trapped in the sea."

A wry smile curved her lips. "Well, not today—even with it

being so beautiful—" She sighed. "But, I'm sure I will swim again. By next summer, a trip to Virginia Beach will find me in the water." She cast him a sideways glance. "After all, it is my love of swimming that helped to save me. If Sophia had been the one to fall overboard or little Rose—" A slight shudder passed through her. She didn't even want to consider the ending of that sentence. "The fact that I have spent so many hours in the water saved me that day," she said, going back to her original thought. "Although I knew my situation wasn't good, I wasn't afraid of the water. Both Sophia and Rose would have been."

She took a deep breath and sighed. "But I do wish I could thank Buddy's and my dolphin." The dog looked up at the mention of his name, and sitting on his hind legs, his tail swished back and forth on the deck's surface like a mop. Elena brought her face close to her canine friend—just as they had been when in the sea together—and she spoke sweet nothings to him while scratching behind his ears.

The affection she shared with the animal passed back and forth between them, a viable thread of devotion, until a deep chuckle emanating from Auhan drew her attentions away. He appeared to be watching something in the distance.

"Well look, there's a dolphin you can thank."

At the thought of a dolphin swimming near the ship, Elena's pulse immediately quickened. But when she saw Auhan's hand pointing upward and not down into the water as she had expected, she blinked and frowned slightly even as she trained her line of vision to follow the direction of his finger.

"Oh!" she exclaimed. "Cloud art." She gazed at the huge cloud in the perfect shape of a dolphin, spreading across the wide expanse of the eastern sky. "One of my favorite things to do when on an ocean voyage is to try and find objects in the shapes of clouds. But this—" she chortled. "This doesn't require any trying." She moved her hand in an arc.

"It looks as if this dolphin has just jumped out of the water and he is only pausing in the sky before returning to the sea." She shook her head. "Amazing."

"Yes," Auhan agreed. "Amazing." Something in his voice alerted Elena to the fact that he wasn't referring to the cloud.

She turned back to him. His eyes, his deep and beautiful eyes as unfathomable as the sea, now regarded her, and she had the crazy but wonderfully disconcerting sensation that he was talking about her. He thought she was amazing.

Feeling flustered and very young and inexperienced, she turned back to the cumulus-cloud dolphin fashioned by the supreme artist. She wanted to keep the mood light. She pointed to the mammal's famous grin, which appeared to extend hundreds of miles across the sky.

"It looks just like our dolphin's smile." She patted Buddy's head, then stayed her hand on the dog to help control the strange, adult feelings now bombarding her.

"How about the giraffe over there?"

Elena turned to see where he pointed. "It is a giraffe," she agreed, even as she cocked her head to the side to accommodate the slightly bent shape of the form. "It's not as easily recognizable as the dolphin, but I definitely see the very long neck of a giraffe. It looks as if it's eating leaves from a tree, a tree made of clouds, of course," she qualified with a smile.

"Your turn," Auhan prompted her to find another shape.

She promptly complied. "Straight ahead. A tiger. You can even see his stripes."

"And how about the motor car over there?" He pointed to a formation that did look remarkably like a Ford Model-T, but Elena only laughed.

"That's the first time I've heard of someone finding an automobile in the clouds."

"Well, why not?" He sighed, almost pensively. "I hope someday to be able to buy one."

She watched him as he looked with true longing at the shape of the vehicle. She had grown up with her father owning automobiles, both in Smyrna and in Washington. Thus, she had never really thought about how some people—young men in particular—might yearn for one. Reaching over, she took his hand in her own.

His fingers wound around hers, and, as on the first morning when she had awakened without a fever, the feel of their hands clasped together felt right; a completion somehow.

He turned to her. A smile crinkled the corners of his eyes—his beautiful eyes, which held secrets she could only guess, but which also held responsive warmth. Slowly, as if from a great distance, she watched as the curve of his mouth moved closer and closer to her. When she felt the warm softness of his lips brush against her cheek, her eyelids fluttered shut, and her entire body tingled as though warm sand trickled across it on a hot summer day.

"Auhan," she whispered his name and swayed toward him, not wanting this closeness to end. He made her feel so womanly. Unlike a moment ago, she didn't feel at all uncomfortable now. His touch made everything right.

"I'm sorry," he murmured, his face just a scant inch from her own. "I shouldn't have—"

She placed her right forefinger against his lips, stilling his words. "Don't." The looks they exchanged roamed one over the other—deep, dark, velvet-brown. Merging. Touching. Meeting. "Don't apologize for something so perfect," she whispered.

"Elena. . ." He transformed her name into a melodious song accompanied by the gentle breeze. A moment before, his lips had touched hers and made the music of her soul leap to glorious life. The movement of his lips touched, tender and soft, against her own. So loving, so warm, so pure was Auhan's kiss, Elena wished it could go on forever. Elena had never been kissed by a man before. Yet she knew, as Auhan's lips left hers, she would never want to kiss another. She had been falling in love with Auhan for the last several days. Now, with his kiss, she was certain. She had stopped "falling" and was wholly, totally "in" love.

"Dear Elena." He caressed the side of her mouth with his fingertip.

"Dear Auhan," she returned. With a sigh as soft as the breeze, she rubbed her cheek against his hand.

After a moment, the most enchanting moment of both their lives, he whispered into her ear, "Dear Elena, where do we go from here?"

She knew what he was asking.

But she also knew she did not want to answer him.

Her answer would be the same as his.

And it was one neither wanted to voice.

Until he made a decision about Christ and resolved his problems, they couldn't take their relationship any further. A wide chasm of theological thoughts and beliefs separated them.

But he was waiting for an answer. She opened her eyes and twisted her head toward the bow of the ship. "How about—New York?"

He laughed.

She laughed back.

He laughed louder, a young, carefree sound she had before never heard issuing from him.

Laughter continued to bubble up and out of her until tears sprang to her eyes.

As they were involved in mutual merriment, a combination

of release and relief, the captain found them.

"Now, what have we here?" His husky voice interrupted them, but Elena could tell from the look he gave them, he was very pleased to find them laughing.

Dabbing her eyes with a handkerchief proffered by Auhan, Elena continued to smile. She couldn't have done otherwise. "Captain," Elena offered her hand to the grandfatherly man as Auhan stood and gave him his chair. "I am just enjoying my first day out in the world again."

" 'Dolphin Girl.' " He reached for her fingers after he sat in the chair volunteered by Auhan. "So I see. And for that I, like Auhan, am very happy." He glanced up at Auhan and nodded his pleasure.

"We were enjoying the cloud art, when. . ." Her cheeks flushed with heat. She suspected that the captain knew they had shared much more than just a fun moment of observation, but she would not enlighten him as to what had further occupied them—their first kiss.

"When," the captain finished for her, "the wonderful, carefree feeling of the day combined with some funny comment to make you both laugh—long and hard." With a grateful heart for his insight and tact, Elena lifted her shoulders in acquiescence. "I'm glad." The older man released her fingers with a gentle squeeze. "You two young people deserve a little fun in life."

Auhan caught Elena in his gaze and they shared a look—that secret look of a close couple who are getting closer by the moment.

The private glance did not escape the notice of the wise, old captain. Between his beard and his mustache, his lips curved upward in acknowledgment before he spoke. "There is a reason I dropped by, other than to receive pleasure out of seeing you out on this beautiful day, my dear," he said to

Elena. "I know your first name, but for my records I need to know your last."

"Yes, of course," she murmured. "My name is Elena Maria Apostologlou."

The captain's brows came together in a thoughtful frown. "Apostologlou?"

"That's right."

"You aren't by any chance related to Andreas Apostologlou, are you?"

A surprised gasp emanated from Elena upon hearing the name. "He was. . .my father."

The captain's sharp intake of breath was his immediate answer. "Your father? Andreas was your father?"

Elena minutely nodded her head.

"Oh, dear girl." The captain reached out for her hands again. He scanned the clean bandages still protecting their burned areas. "Auhan told me you lost your father the last night you were in Smyrna. I just didn't realize your father was Andreas." Visibly shaken by the news, the captain inhaled in deep, controlling breaths. "I am so sorry. I knew your father well. He was one of the most honest, fair men I ever had the privilege of carrying cargo for, not once, but many times." He gave a poignant smile.

"I always wondered if his name might have had something to do with the forming of his character. Doesn't the first part of your last name mean 'apostle' while the ending denotes someone coming from the Constantinople area of the world?"

"That's right," she concurred in breathless wonder. She was amazed by the captain's knowledge. Most people, even those familiar with things Hellenic, didn't realize that Greek names normally had interesting meanings and, quite often, Christian ones; hence their many letters. Her father had taught her to be very proud of her long, very old and significant last name.

The captain took another deep breath and said, "If ever a man lived up to his name, it was your father. He was truly like an apostle of Christ."

"Thank you, Captain," Elena responded. "I always thought so too."

"Many did, my dear. Many did. If there were more men—more Christians—in the world like your father, wars would never take place."

&

Auhan watched as a solemn Elena nodded her head. The captain's reference pointed out something that had always bothered him about Christianity and was a major stumbling block to his believing in God as revealed by Jesus Christ. Christians fighting Christians seemed like a contradiction to him, and he was beginning to think the captain felt the same way. It was the second time the man had mentioned something similar. Auhan wanted to pursue the subject further. But when he saw the poignant expression shadowing Elena's features at the captain's mention of her father, he held his tongue. This was her day. Her time to enjoy. He almost wished the captain hadn't asked for her last name. Serious topics had no place in today's magic.

But he didn't fault the captain. Who would have thought the giving of her name would have caused the atmosphere to turn so heavy? Auhan wanted to change it back to the light and carefree one of before. Looking up in the sky, he knew how.

"Elena," he interrupted the weighty silence. "Why don't you show the captain your dolphin."

The quick smile that readily split across her face told of her relief in changing the subject. She launched into a lighthearted explanation about her wishing to thank the dolphin who had saved her and Buddy and how they had found the one she now pointed out in the clouds.

Watching her animated, intelligent face, Auhan knew they would discuss serious topics again.

But not today.

He looked out over the calm sea and smiled as she and the captain continued to chat.

No. Today was not the day to speak to Elena about anything but happy things. Now was a time of celebration, to rejoice in her being alive.

Reaching for the teapot, he poured all three of them a cup of the brew while listening to Elena as her bubbly laughter filled the air.

It was music of the most excellent kind, and Auhan breathed in deeply of the moment.

eleven

*The people answered him, We have heard out of the law
that Christ abideth for ever: and how sayest thou,
The Son of man must be lifted up? who is this Son of man?
Then Jesus said unto them, Yet a little while is the light
with you. Walk while ye have the light, lest darkness come
upon you: for he that walketh in darkness knoweth not
whither he goeth. While ye have light, believe in the light,
that ye may be the children of light.*
John 12:34–36

As Auhan stood at the railing of the ship late that night, he
heard the deep sounds of the captain's voice coming from
behind him. "When I consider thy heavens, the work of thy
fingers, the moon and the stars, which thou hast ordained;
what is man that thou art mindful of him?"

The poetic words surprised Auhan. They were beautiful;
but even more, they expressed exactly what he had been
thinking as he gazed out over the star-filled sky of the soft,
North Atlantic night. What was man compared to such awe-
some worlds as those that sparkled above him? And even
more, why should Auhan even expect a God of such vastness
to care about insignificant, little, warring humans?

Auhan turned to the captain as he came to stand beside
him. "How did you know my exact thoughts?"

"It's what all young men who are thinkers consider when
they look out over a night such as this," the captain replied
and motioned to the heavens above.

Auhan turned back to the night scene. The sky was so full of stars, it looked like a blanket of soft, white cotton had been placed over a blue-black bed of deepest velvet.

"Thinker?" he questioned. His brother was the thinker, not he.

"Aren't you?" the captain challenged.

Auhan blew air out from between his teeth. "I have been considering things a great deal lately," he admitted in his heavily accented but one hundred percent grammatically correct English.

"If that makes me a thinker, then I guess I am," he replied and paused. "It's just—" he began, but stopped and sighed, then sighed again.

"Go on," the captain prompted.

Auhan lifted his hand and nodded heavenward. "Is God mindful of man?" he asked, using the exact words the captain had just spoken.

"Let's finish seeing what the rest of the eighth psalm says." The captain spoke with love in his voice and seemed to worship the creator as he gazed out over the infinite sky and recited the scripture. The fact that the captain so obviously believed every word he spoke touched a cord deep within Auhan's soul.

" 'What is man, that thou art mindful of him?' " the captain repeated, " 'and the son of man, that thou visitest him? For thou hast made him a little lower than the angels, and hast crowned him with glory and honour. Thou madest him to have dominion over the works of thy hands; thou hast put all things under his feet: All sheep and oxen, yea, and the beasts of the field; The fowl of the air, and the fish of the sea, and whatsoever passeth through the paths of the seas.' "

The captain paused as emotion filled his throat. Then, with a resounding tone, he finished his recitation. " 'O LORD our

LORD, how excellent is thy name in all the earth!' "

Silence settled between the two men, yet it was a friendly one. Comforting. Auhan really didn't understand everything the captain said—he wondered about this "son of man"—but the fact that the words meant so much to this man of authority whom Auhan had grown to greatly admire during the past two weeks gave him cause to ponder.

"I must admit, Captain," he spoke after a thoughtful moment. "Between watching how you conduct your life and Elena hers and now seeing the change in my own mother, the Christian faith is beginning to seem very—," he paused and scanned his brain for the correct word, "—interesting to me."

"But?" the captain asked, and Auhan turned to him in surprise. "There is something which you wish to ask. I sensed it earlier today when on deck with our 'Dolphin Girl.' " Again, the captain's ability to note Auhan's mental musings impressed him. He didn't even try to deny his questions.

"I didn't want to say anything then." He shrugged his shoulders. "Elena needed happiness today. Nothing else."

"I agree. She needed today. But tomorrow or the next you might ask her anything you so desire. If she is anything like her father," he paused and chuckled, "and after having dolphins come to her rescue, I have no doubt she is—you'll find her to be a young lady of much understanding and knowledge. What we have seen in her so far is just the beginning, I'm sure. You will do well to bring your questions to her. The communication will draw you closer together. That's the key to a good relationship with another person—especially a young woman with whom you are growing very fond."

Auhan smiled into the darkness. He couldn't see the other man's eyes, but from the timber in his voice he knew they had to be twinkling like the giant star Antares. He needn't even attempt to deny his feelings. "I do like her. Very much."

"Then don't be afraid to talk to her."

"I'm not. We've already shared some interesting conversations. But, I wanted today to be special for her, free from anything save good thoughts," he repeated his earlier words.

"Both smart and considerate of you." The captain acknowledged. "But," he asked after a quiet moment, "might I help you with your questions or at least one of them now?"

Auhan nodded and breathed deeply of the clean, ocean-scented night before plunging into the profound waters of a theological discussion. "Like I said, your faith is beginning to seem very interesting to me." He turned to the captain. "But what about Christians fighting Christians?"

He doubted anyone could help him with his other questions, such as how the Christian God could allow little babies to be killed and thrown into mass graves. . .or how he could permit Elena and others like her to go through the tortures they had just experienced during the destruction of their city. No. No one could answer such tormenting questions.

Elena probably could. He frowned as the thought zipped through his brain, and he spoke quickly to cover both the surprise and unease it brought to him.

"I can somewhat understand why groups of diverse religious backgrounds might war with one another. It isn't right," he qualified, "but, I can see how so much divides and it might happen, such as with the Greeks and the Turks." He took a deep breath. "But Christians against Christians? Such a thing doesn't make any sense to me at all, and wasn't that what the Great War was all about?" The conflict had always presented a major stumbling block to Auhan's belief in the authenticity of Christianity.

"No, the Great War was never about Christians fighting Christians," the captain was quick to refute. "Rather, it was about imperialism and economics and greed; about groups of people wanting more than another, an age-old problem between humans and one not inclusive only to those who call themselves Christians."

But if Auhan was ever to believe in the God of his ancestors, he needed more convincing evidence than this. The captain's answer seemed too pat. He pressed on. "But the Germans, Austrians, and Hungarians are all Christians—and on the other side, the English, the French, and the Russians. These groups fought one another and brought other nations into the fray as well," Auhan pressed on.

"For the most part, yes, those nations mentioned are predominantly Christian. The captain didn't try to refute the commonly held fact. "But what people forget, and some such as yourself don't even realize, is that Christianity is not a huge group of people who simply *call* themselves Christians. Rather, Christianity is about Christ. If a person wonders about Christianity, he is not to look at me or at that lovely girl sleeping below or at any other person or nation of people in this world. Only at the man—the God—from where we get the 'Christ' of the word 'Christ-ianity.' Christ is the perfect one. Not me. Not Elena. Not the English or the French. Not the Germans or the Austrians. Not the Hungarians or the Italians or the Greeks or any other race of people. Christ is perfect and just and everything good in the world, the only true good to have ever existed.

"And too," the captain continued, "many people who say they are Christians have no idea what being a Christian really means. A Christian isn't a group or a denomination to which one belongs or a set of traditions one follows in order to go to heaven. Rather, a Christian is one who has made a decision to turn from a life of sin and has asked Christ to help as he or she seeks to live a holy, loving lifestyle."

"My mother made a choice to be a Christian. Is she, then,

a true Christian?" Auhan asked.

"It would seem so. But even still, Christ is the one you should look to. Not your mother. Because no matter how closely a person follows the life of Christ, we all fall short. We aren't perfect. Oh, we often get better and better as we study and learn and pray—we should actually—but still sometimes a Christian might do something that makes another wonder about Christianity and say, such as yourself, 'Well, if the Germans and the English are fighting each other, then what good is Christianity?' But Christianity is not the English or the Germans or the Greeks or the Austrians or the Americans or the Hungarians. Christianity is Christ."

"So, you are saying I shouldn't look at another person when judging whether to believe the message of Christ or not?"

"Not entirely. You can look at Elena or at your mother or at me and wonder if the way we live our lives—with the Lord Jesus Christ at the very center of our being—is something you would like to experience for yourself. But if we do something you don't like, you shouldn't let that be the measure by which you judge Christianity."

"Then, Jesus Christ is the—measure?" Auhan asked. He wasn't too sure about the meaning of the word "measure" as used in this context, but he guessed it to be something similar to a musical measure and that the captain meant it was a criterion to follow.

"That's right." The other man paused. "You see, Son, even if there were no Christians in the world—no people who believed the message Jesus Christ came to earth to give— that would not negate the truth of His message or of His redemptive act. He is. Jesus Christ is God's Son whether you believe it or I believe it or anybody in this world does. His truth is not dependent on people's belief." He paused. "But conversely, our salvation *is* dependent on His truth. He came to earth for us. Like a parent wanting to rescue His child, He came to earth to save us."

"But why then should Christians fight one another?" Auhan went back to his original question.

"Personally," the captain breathed out a heavy sigh, "I don't believe people who have made a conscious effort to follow Christ do make war on one another. I'm not saying believing Christians won't serve their country and fight in wars, for that comes under the scriptural directive to follow the laws of our individual countries."

"So, what you're saying is that only non-Christians are behind wars?" Auhan persisted, somewhat appalled. He didn't know if he agreed with that idea. In fact, he was almost certain he didn't.

The captain grimaced. "I guess it sounds that way. Maybe that is what I personally believe. Any sort of official state-ment to the effect might cause lots of problems. So, let me qualify myself a bit." He paused and seemed to think a moment. "If by non-Christian you include in that group peo-ple who are only traditional Christians—people who call themselves Christians because their parents were, and theirs before them, and so on back into time, yet who have never made a personal, conscious choice to believe Christ's mes-sage—then yes." He shook his head.

"That's not to say those born in the tradition of Christian-ity, such as myself, don't have a great advantage over those who are not. They do. But that advantage also brings respon-sibility—the responsibility not to take one's faith for granted and the responsibility to teach others. Christ demands a response from each person, whether he or she comes from a family of believers or not."

When the captain finished, Auhan took a deep breath, then blew it out from between his teeth in a half-whistle. "That's a lot to consider, Sir."

The captain patted him on the back. "Well now, that's why God gave humans good brains. We have the ability to think through things. Personally, I think He gave us our brains in order for us to use them to find Him. Unfortunately, most don't take the time to do so. But I'll tell you something else, Son. When we say 'yes' to Christ and the Spirit of God moves into our hearts to live within us, He gives us a whole new life. When the learned Nicodemus—" The captain paused when a sailor approached.

"What is it, Sailor?"

"Excuse me, Sir, but you are needed above."

The captain nodded, dismissing the sailor, then turned back to Auhan. "I'm sorry, Son, but duty calls." As he spoke, he straightened his cap and prepared to leave. "Just remember this. When you answer 'yes' to Jesus, 'yes' that you believe Him, then you are reborn a new man. A new man in Christ. And He is able to give you that rebirth because He is God, not just a prophet of God. Think about it." The captain turned on his heels and walked away with the clipped, authoritative steps of a man whose mind was already on the job before him.

Auhan turned to look out at the starlit sea again. Somehow, it seemed to be even brighter than a few moments before.

*Rebirth. . .*the word replayed in his mind as Auhan breathed deeply of the ocean air. *Was it possible?*

He smiled. He was beginning to think that many things were more possible than he had ever considered before.

&

Two days passed—glorious days in which Auhan and Elena laughed and talked, looked for art in the clouds, and just enjoyed being a young and happy, seemingly carefree couple.

The third day Elena told Auhan she felt strong enough to walk out to the deck on her own. Even though he missed the closeness of carrying her, he thrilled to see her renewed strength and energy. He discovered a new joy in having her by his side, of using his strong arms to support her, of just being a couple perambulating together. He hadn't anticipated such a pleasant bonus. Auhan had often seen happy couples strolling along as they were doing now, and he had always thought those other couples were a bit foolish. Perhaps he had been the foolish one.

As he guided Elena toward the canopy, she motioned to the glorious day which once again surrounded their ship and exclaimed, "Oh, Auhan, when the sun sat that day when I was in the sea, I didn't know if I would ever see the world like this again." She placed her hand on her dog's head and sank into her seat. "Except for Buddy and the dolphin, I don't know if I would have made it." Auhan's jaw clenched upon hearing the slight catch in Elena's voice, and he reached out to instinctively ruffle Buddy's soft fur.

Even though the captain's explanation of a few nights ago about Christians fighting Christians made sense, Auhan still had a hard time with the suffering that the millions of Christians of Asia Minor—and particularly this woman who had become very dear to him—had gone through. How could God allow it? It was totally beyond Auhan's thinking that Elena could still consider God as her friend. He didn't see how she could think God actually loved her after He had allowed her to be so grievously hurt, both physically and mentally.

"I'm so sorry you had to go through all that Elena." He seated himself across from her. "If I could have prevented it, I would have." Her eyebrows lifted in question when he put emphasis on the pronouns.

"What are you saying?" Her lips formed a firm line across her face. "That God didn't prevent it?"

She knew him too well. He didn't even try to deny it. How could he? It was exactly what he meant. "That's right," he agreed. In spite of everything, all Auhan could conclude was that God hadn't helped her just as he hadn't helped all those people—those Christians—in that mass grave or others like it.

"If God is your friend, then why did He allow you to suffer in the sea on top of all that you had already endured?" Doubt flavored his words.

"God didn't bring the suffering, Auhan," she sighed, and he detected a weary note to her voice. "Men did. Men who made wrong choices." She raised her bandage-covered hands in the air even as the pitch of her voice rose. "It amazes me how God is always blamed for the mistakes and meanness of people."

The thought caught Auhan's attention, and he would have given it more consideration if she hadn't totally staggered him with her next statement. "But even with what I went through, God did bring good to me." Her voice softened, and, as he wondered what good she could possibly mean, she reached out and brushed the tips of her fingers across his right cheek with her right hand. "He brought you to me, dear Auhan," she whispered, and her eyes became as soft as liquid gold. "And I am beginning to think a day spent in the sea was worth meeting you."

His gaze narrowed. That was the last thing he had expected her to say, and he didn't know how to respond. Or how he felt. Wonderful? Frightened? Flabbergasted? To think that such a girl would think such a nice thing about him. The realization was almost too much.

She shrugged her shoulders as though embarrassed by his sudden quietness, but she continued with a determined tilt to her jaw. "Maybe for us to meet was the reason I was 'allowed' to fall off that rescue ship, Auhan."

Auhan looked away from her honest eyes and out at the mighty ocean. Quietly, with his voice as smooth as the water's surface, he asked, "Do you really think God let you fall overboard so that we could meet?" To part of him, it seemed totally absurd. To another part, both amazing and wonderful.

"It's possible," Elena admitted after a moment, and he let out a deep breath, one that carried a large weight with it.

"I do have feelings for you, Elena." He wouldn't even try to deny them. He wasn't sure when they had started—probably while he stood on deck that night and watched the sailors pull her out of the sea with all those dolphins jumping around her. "But, because I haven't felt anything but anger and bitterness for so long, I don't know if I can do anything with these feelings—if I can offer you anything," he qualified. "I'm crippled, Elena. In my mind, my soul, I'm crippled."

It was more than he had admitted out loud to his parents or even to himself before.

"Dear Auhan." She looked at him with such compassion, he felt as though she had reached out and caressed him. She had. She had caressed his hurting, weeping soul.

"Don't you know, until God lives in our hearts, we are all crippled?"

He stood up so suddenly, Buddy growled a sound of fear and confusion, and Elena rested a reassuring hand on the dog's golden head to reassure him. "God! Why would I want such an impotent God living within me? You don't know what I've seen. The wicked things I've seen done to God's so-called people, even while they called out to Him for help." He nearly spat the words, and he saw the horror of what he had seen reflected in her eyes.

❧

She recognized his stare of terror-filled panic. She had seen painfully similar abominations in Smyrna. The horrors would take control of her too. If she let them.

But a fresh, sudden thought, a terrible thought, went through Elena's head, and she licked her cotton-dry lips. "Auhan, while fleeing Smyrna, I overheard a group of Turkish soldiers taunting a family they were about to murder, 'Why doesn't your God save you now?' they had snarled out." Her face became pale as she remembered back. She had blocked the wretched scene from her mind until this moment—until Auhan's statement about other Christians in other parts of the empire calling out to God triggered the memory. And her blood ran cold once again.

Auhan fell to his knees beside her. Remorse covered his features. "I'm so sorry, Elena. I shouldn't have marred this moment with such talk."

She ignored his placating words. "Are you taunting me with the same question?"

Auhan's face turned ashen. "No, Elena, no." He shook his head back and forth absolutely denying it. "I didn't. I mean, I never—" He buried his face in his hands. "Elena, no. I'm not taunting you. Please, you must believe me," he pleaded. "I'm just wondering why? Why would God allow so many thousands of His people to die? Why didn't He rescue them? Why did He allow deportations that killed thousands of mothers and their children? Thousands of babies." Babies in blue sweaters.

Elena looked out into the still sea. But she wasn't seeing the mighty Atlantic Ocean or looking for the still unseen freedom-loving shores of her other home, of America. Rather, she was seeing the fleets of Western ships filled with Christians as they floated in the harbor of Smyrna a couple of weeks ago. They had done nothing—absolutely nothing—to help bring the people, the remnant of believers from one of the oldest Christian lands in the world, to safety.

In mute dismay, Elena shook her head.

God had sent help to the Christians of the Smyrna Protectorate. He had sent help in the form of the strongest nations on earth—and even that of her other country, America. Those nations, filled with Christians, simply sat and watched as their allies, their Christian brothers and sisters, were slaughtered. Not until the Greeks and Armenians were trapped between the burning city and the deep, wind-churned harbor did some—some, but not all—start to help. But that was after thousands had been murdered in cold blood. Her father included.

How evil had laughed in the inferno of those hours.

She could still hear its awful sound. Among all the cries of agony, torture, blood being spilled, evil's cackles, snarls, and snickers still resounded in her head.

Her body shook.

But she could feel Auhan's warm arms as they enfolded her, could smell his wonderful scent, and could feel his heart—his life—beating against her palm.

Then, she heard his voice. He was calling out to her.

"Elena, Elena," he repeated her name over and over. "Dear," he was rubbing her face. "Please, Darling."

That endearment got through to her. Still plagued with horror-filled visions of her city's indigenous population being slaughtered, she turned to him and picked up the fabric of their conversation as if there had been no interval.

"Tell me, Auhan," she said, her voice flat but demanding. "What exactly do you believe about God?"

His eyes reddened and filled with unshed tears as he shook his head negatively. "That is not something. . .you. . .want. . . to know," he rasped, his voice sounding scraped and stripped.

"Maybe not," she admitted. "But it's something I have to know before I can help you."

He gave a bitter laugh. "No one can help me."

"God can."

"God is impotent," he spat in reply.

"Is that what you believe?" If that were it, she would deal with it. But somehow, she felt certain there was more to it than that. To say God was impotent was just a battle cry.

Muscles twitched along his jaw, and she could see a war raging within his soul. Like Smyrna's war, like all wars, it was ugly. Hideous.

"I was a Turkish soldier," he ground out after a moment. "Doesn't that bother you at all?"

"Did you kill any civilians?" she asked, her voice barely above a whisper.

"No." He shook his head from side to side in fierce denial. "Never."

"Then," she paused and moistened her lips, "perhaps you were as much a victim as I?"

He shook his head. "No. Not a victim like you." He paused. "I held a gun."

She flinched. "But you didn't use it on civilians?" she questioned again.

He shook his head again in adamant refute. And she believed him. Totally. She hadn't forgotten he had been a Turkish soldier. Not once. Not even as she had been falling in love with him had she forgotten. But she had been certain too that he had never hurt a defenseless person. Having him volunteer the information was all the proof she needed. Putting the unpleasant facts behind her, as she had so many other things, she nodded and returned to her original question. "Auhan, please tell me what you believe, what you truly believe. You have rightly admitted you are crippled. I want to help. But I have to know what you believe in order to do so."

He shook his head as a tear fell from the corner of each of his red eyes.

"Auhan." She leaned toward him and wiped his teardrops

away. "I know you weren't taunting me with your question." Her countenance and her voice offered him sweet assurance. "I understand. If you'll let me, I'll do my best to help you discover the answers to all your haunting questions."

☙

Auhan looked at her, really looked into her eyes. He knew that she wouldn't stop pressing him for an answer until he told her. He also knew his trying to convince himself that she wasn't strong enough to know the truth was a lie. She was the strongest person he knew.

"Please, Auhan. Not knowing is the hardest thing for me," she said, reading his mind as easily as if it had been an open book.

In slow acquiescence, he nodded his head. He could understand her need to probe. He would feel the same way if the roles were reversed. With lips that barely moved, he opened his heart, his dark and cold dungeon of a heart, for the first time in over a year.

"I believe. . ." He shook his head as the somber words left his mouth. He didn't want to speak. He knew with their voicing, he would destroy any chance of a life together with her. He sighed and began again. "I believe that evil rules this world, Elena. Not God. Evil."

Slowly, a smile, a sad one, but still a smile, touched her colorless lips. Auhan never felt more shocked in his life when she replied, "Dear Auhan, you are absolutely correct."

twelve

*And out of the ground made the LORD God to grow every
tree that is pleasant to the sight, and good for food;
the tree of life also in the midst of the garden,
and the tree of knowledge of good and evil.*
Genesis 2:9

*Blessed are they that do his commandments,
that they may have right to the tree of life,
and may enter in through the gates into the city.*
Revelation 22:14

"Evil does rule this world, Auhan. And yet God is still sovereign." She looked out over the mighty body of water and smiled a sweet smile of hope.

Auhan shook his head as if to clear his confusion. "That's a contradiction, Elena." The calmness of his voice amazed him. He felt anything but calm.

Her eyes held not the slightest glimmer of doubt when she looked at him. "No, it's no contradiction. Although God is sovereign, that is to say, He possesses supreme power, evil does indeed have a sphere of influence, a rule, here on earth." She frowned in thought.

"You see, Auhan, that's exactly why God sent His Son to earth. To break the hold the evil one has over people."

He looked at her in amazement. "How can you say such a thing? How can you even believe it? Especially after what you have just lived through?" He made an ill-tempered grunt.

"*Barely* lived through, I should say."

"Because it's true," she insisted. Even though he shook his head in disagreement, she continued. "Auhan, we don't know when Satan became God's enemy. We don't even know when he, the most glorious of all God's angels, fell into sin. But we do know evil came into this world through his lying, tricking words."

She leaned forward as though to punctuate the importance of her words. "We read in the Bible, in the third chapter of Genesis. 'And he said unto the woman, Yea, hath God said, Ye shall not eat of every tree of the garden?' " Elena's eyes widened with the question.

"The conniving serpent had expertly planted the seed of doubt within her innocent mind, and the poor woman replied, 'We may eat of the fruit of the trees of the garden: But of the fruit of the tree which is in the midst of the garden, God hath said, Ye shall not eat of it, neither shall ye touch it, lest ye die.' "

Auhan made an impatient motion with his hands. "This is just a children's story."

Elena vigorously nodded her head up and down, and she surprised him again by agreeing with him. "That's right, it is! It's God's story to His children—to us."

Auhan was too bewildered by her response to reply. In truth, the thought was an amazing one. God's story to His children? His children? Was that what the Bible was?

"How do you suppose the evil one responded to God's words as repeated by the woman?" Elena didn't wait for a response, but answered her own question.

"With a nice big contradiction, that's how. He told her, 'Ye shall not surely die: For God doth know that in the day ye eat thereof, then your eyes shall be opened, and ye shall be as gods, knowing good and evil.' " Elena paused and looked deeply at Auhan. "What a lie. Evil was not something we ever had to know, needed to know about." She gazed toward the eastern horizon, while Auhan looked into his soul.

How often had he wondered why? Why had he had to learn about evil at that grave? It was an amazing thought to hear Elena say God hadn't wanted him to know about such depravity. God had never intended for him to come to that moment in his life. Neither had He wanted Elena to face evil in her home city. But what made their reaction to evil so different? The darkness of it all had nearly killed him, whereas Elena, in spite of everything, still shone with hope and light.

He found himself listening with rapt attention as she continued. "Believe me, evil is not something we want, and God never wanted us to have to know it or to have to fight it in our lives," she repeated with fervor.

"Even though He would not keep its knowledge from us if we so chose to have it, He didn't want us to know it. No more than your parents or mine ever wanted us, as their children, to eat or do something that was bad for us, which would cause us harm or even death." Her words sparked with passion as she spoke.

Auhan couldn't help but think of his sister. She had been warned by their parents, as had all three of them, not to go too close to the water. She had disobeyed, died, and brought immeasurable pain upon them all.

In spite of his disbelief, Auhan found himself interested in what she was saying. That she believed it made it important to him. "You know, there is something most people don't notice when reading about the fall of man in Genesis. The Bible tells us there were two trees in the middle of the garden."

"Two?" He frowned. He didn't recall ever hearing this fact. He'd only heard about the one tree.

She nodded her head. "Right next to the tree of the

knowledge of good and evil stood the tree of life."

"The tree of life?" He was certain he had never heard about that tree.

She nodded her head. "God didn't warn the man and the woman not to eat from the tree of life. Before they disobeyed God, they could have eaten from it at any time they so desired."

Auhan felt Elena might be hitting upon a topic few people ever considered. She definitely had his interest. It was as if, for the first time, everything—all his thoughts and questions— were coming into accord. One of the things he loved most about playing the violin was tuning it, something he had never been able to do with his life, not even before the war. He continued to listen, as she seemed to speak one more remarkable word upon another, words he wanted to hear with a desire stronger than any yearning he had ever felt—even stronger than his love of playing the violin. He longed to believe. And her words seemed to be answering the fervent hope of his soul.

"The woman and the man disobeyed the only command- ment God had, up to that time, given to them. The only one. Don't you think, Auhan, God gave them this one command because it was important to their welfare? He loved them so much, He didn't want them to have to deal with evil. God had created a world apart from evil. A world of freedom. Humans needed only to trust God's commandment, have faith in His judgment. God gave the command in order for the tree of human history to remain unmarred by the evil one. So simple. As simple as a child listening to—or ignoring—his parents." She sighed with a sound that held the sadness of the ages.

Auhan pursed his lips in contemplation. "But if God is sovereign and all-knowing, surely He knew what would hap- pen—how they would choose. Couldn't He have prevented it?" Elena's face brightened at his inquiry.

"I believe even though He knew how His creation would choose when confronted with the evil one, the pain that choice would bring to Him was still worth all the joy." She smiled and swept away from her face the strands of hair that the gentle breeze had pushed into her eyes. "Kind of like earthly parents. All people are wise enough to know that, although children are a blessing, in many cases they bring much pain to their parents' hearts. But even with knowing this, people still want children. Yearn for them. We have children in the hope they will become wonderful human beings. Yet, God knew, even before He created us, exactly how many would actually turn out to bring joy to Him. And, even though He knew not all of us would make the right choice when confronted with the question of obedience, God considered His resulting suffering and pain worthwhile."

Auhan still had a hard time believing that God considered humans as His children, and he wasn't quite sure about the "choice" Elena referred to, but he didn't interrupt her with his doubts. He wanted to hear her out. The information her brain contained fascinated him, and, well, something was stirring within him. He wasn't sure what it was exactly, only that it was something nice, something bright, as if, for the first time ever, the music of his soul was beginning to play to the correct melody.

"To answer the second part of your question, God couldn't have prevented our choice, not without taking away human volition, that is, our humanness. We have to be held accountable for our actions. The decision made by the man and woman gave evil the right to invade the perfect world God had made for them, and they immediately stopped living in the light of God, and darkness revealed them."

"Darkness revealed them?" Auhan questioned the seeming contradiction, and Elena nodded in response.

"Upon looking at one another, they saw they were naked—because for the first time in their existence, they were. Man and woman, God's created children, no longer had the 'clothing' of God's light to cover them."

Auhan looked at her in amazement. Maybe that first man and woman no longer had the light of God's "clothing," but Elena certainly did. Even when sick in bed, she had looked as though God's light had been wrapped around her like an exquisite mantle. He knew now it was this very thing that had made him take note of her from the beginning, that had gotten his attention when nothing else could.

Elena was clothed in the light of God's love.

His eyes widened.

Where had that thought come from? He had never thought such a thing before. But, to his amazement, he didn't want to stop. He felt something not only stir, but now jump, within his soul. It was as if he were coming alive after having been dead. All he wanted was to hear more.

"Go on." He heard his voice speak the words, but he didn't feel like the words came from him any longer. Yet, even that made him glad. He didn't like the person he had become, a person without hope, without love, without light, a person who believed evil was in control of the world.

When Auhan looked at Elena, her eyes sparkled as though she too sensed something was different about him. He wondered if she realized that an entirely new feeling now radiated from him. For the first time, he felt his spirit was in one accord with hers.

"Even though His children disobeyed, He was already working on a plan to make things right again. Before we even leave the third chapter of the book of Genesis, God spoke Himself into the world. He spoke Himself into the very fabric of the world's future population so that He could act and solve the problem of the separation between Himself—a holy God—and sinful man. God came into the world through the right door—the door of human bloodline—and He offered Himself to correct the rift standing between Him and the people He longed to call His children. Jesus Christ—the Son of man—"

"Jesus Christ *was* the Son of man?" Auhan interrupted her, remembering the verses the captain had recited the starry night on deck. If Christ was the same Son of man he had referred to, it certainly explained a lot.

"Jesus Christ *is* the Son of man." Elena corrected his tense and continued. "He was born a human baby. He lived among us, revealed God—who is Himself—to us, taught us, and then hung on that cross, died on that cross, and took our punishment for all the wrongs we have ever done, will ever do," she qualified, "in order to make everything right. He did this to prevent mankind from being under the dominion of the evil one any longer. It's done. The work is complete. All we have to do—all anyone of any race anywhere in the world has to do—is to tell Him we are sorry for our sins and believe Jesus is who He, Himself, said He is—God."

Auhan dropped his gaze and studied the floor while he concentrated on her words.

"If Jesus' sinless life doesn't prove to you who He is, if all the prophecies about Him don't prove it, if all of His miracles don't prove it, if His teachings don't prove it, if His dying on the cross and then being resurrected doesn't prove it to you. . ." She paused and touched her hand to where his heart beat beneath his jacket and vest. "Then, please, let the Comforter, the One Jesus sent when He ascended to heaven, the One who can live within your heart, prove it to you. It's all real. It's all true. It's God's story of redemption to His children—the most fantastic 'children's' story ever penned. Jesus is the one who conquered evil. He is the one who provides a way for us to reach the other tree in the middle of the garden again—the tree of life. Because of man's bad choice, evil does influence this world, Auhan. But. . . ," she paused, and Auhan looked up to see her smile. "God still rules supreme."

Hot tears slid from the corners of Auhan's eyes and down his face. He didn't even try to wipe the tears away. Instead, he reached for her hands and intertwined her fingers in his. Speaking softly but with sincere desire, he said, "Elena, I want to be a part of such a belief. What do I have to do?"

She cried out, squeezing his hands in hers. "Oh, dear Auhan, just believe. Just believe that Jesus Christ—God's Son—came to earth to save you from the grips of the evil one. Just believe He came to pay the price of your guilt in order that you might be born a whole new person."

At those words, his shoulders heaved, and for the first time since he was a little boy, sobs, great, big, heaving sobs, erupted from his body. He cried for himself. He cried for what he had seen. He cried for Elena and her family and the thousands of families in Smyrna and in Asia Minor. He cried for the baby in the blue sweater. And as his sobs subsided, he prayed and asked the Lord Jesus to live within his heart.

Auhan believed. He was a new person in Christ. His desire to be reborn had just come true. And he knew he would never relinquish his new life. Not ever.

thirteen

*Rejoice in the L*ORD*,*
*O ye righteous. . .Praise the L*ORD *with harp:*
sing unto him with the psaltery
and an instrument of ten strings.
Sing unto him a new song;
play skilfully with a loud noise.
Psalm 33:1–3

After Auhan's birth into the kingdom of God, Elena and Auhan sat on the deck for hours in the pure lighting of the ocean sun. They talked and laughed and grew closer and closer to one another and, as a couple, closer to God. They were now both members of the same spiritual family, God's family; and on that seafaring deck, their love blossomed into the most beautiful of blooms.

By the time the sun sat very low in the sky, Elena knew she would spend her life together with this man. She didn't want to leave the magic of the deck, but her body was still on the mend, and Auhan insisted she needed her rest. Before she went to bed, however, they agreed on one more thing Auhan needed to do on this most remarkable day.

The pitter-patter of the dog proceeded them into the cabin. *Anne* Fatima stopped in the motion of slinging her shawl around her shoulders when Auhan guided Elena over the threshold. "I was just about to come looking for you two," she exclaimed. Dropping her shawl onto a bunk, she quickly crossed over to Elena. With concern etching lines in her face,

Fatima placed her hand against her forehead while Elena waited patiently. The dear woman sighed, and the lines left her face when she seemed assured that Elena's temperature was normal. *Anne* Fatima turned back to her son, obviously intent on admonishing him for keeping her out so long. But, *Anne* Fatima stayed her words of reproach when she saw Auhan reach for his violin case. A gasp escaped the devoted mother, and her gaze searched the cabin for her husband.

Elena watched as Suleiman rose from the side of his bunk and reached for his wife's outstretched hand. Elena watched as, together, they considered their son. Lines of wonder painted their classical features when Auhan gently, almost reverently, laid the leather case on his bunk, unlatched it with great care, and lifted the lid.

Reaching down, he ran his fingertips over the smooth varnish of the meticulously crafted instrument. Elena thought he looked as though he were greeting an old friend. Her eyes widened when she looked closely at the red-toned violin. Auhan had told her earlier that his violin was a very special instrument—a gift from a very old, childless, Greek merchant who had recognized Auhan's great talent.

But the instrument before her eyes far surpassed anything she had envisioned. She didn't claim to know much about violins. However, she had seen a good number of them up close when musicians performed in her father's salon in Smyrna. With certainty, she knew this one before her now was of exceptional quality. Very likely it was a sixteenth-century creation from an Italian school. *Perhaps, from the workshop of Stradivari himself,* she thought with a tingle of excitement.

Taking meticulous care, Auhan lifted the intricately crafted violin from its velvet bed. For a moment he just cradled the instrument in his arms as he would a baby. He cast a conspiratorial smile in Elena's direction, and her heart beat glad within her chest. Then, he nestled the violin beneath his chin. He started plucking at the strings to tune it, and he finished the task with such quick and expert ease, he looked like he had done the task as recently as the day before. Elena moved to stand beside Fatima as Auhan turned to his parents. Picking up the bow, he touched it to the strings. He paused and presented them all with a smile so full of light, they all answered with matching grins.

Then.

Then.

Auhan made music.

The most wonderful, the most meaningful rendition of Beethoven's "Ode to Joy" Elena had ever heard came forth from the movement of Auhan's hands, from his body, from the music within his soul.

Auhan played and played. He bobbed and bowed. He was one with the instrument, one with the melody. The sound seemed to transcend the physical as sweet music rose above the din of the ship's engines and floated out over the ocean to God above.

Tears ran down Elena's face, down his parents' too. And when Auhan played the last glorious note and the final sound drifted out of the cabin into the never-never land of silent-but-remembered melodies, Auhan looked over at Elena.

For a long moment, they gazed into each other's eyes. Words weren't necessary to convey the hope, the love filling their hearts.

At Elena's gentle nod, Auhan, still holding the violin in his hands, walked over to his mother and father. "*Anne, Baba.* No more tears." He reached into his pocket and pulled out a clean handkerchief, then handed it to his mother. "No more tears for me. I am healed."

He looked down at the cross that hung from his mother's neck.

"The cross of Jesus Christ has healed me; it has made me whole. Made me well. Made me—" He paused as emotion clogged his throat. "Made me into a whole new man."

Fatima cried out, a mother's sweet cry filled with pure joy. Elena watched as the woman hugged her child close. "Oh, Auhan, my dear, dear boy." She pulled back and looked up at her husband.

"Suleiman?" she asked. "I believe in the God of our ancestors. Our son believes now too. But what about you?"

He looked between his son and his wife and then shifted his gaze to Elena. He ran his large hand over the short, silky locks of her golden hair and cleared the emotion from his throat before testing his little-used voice. "E-le-na," he stammered. He paused and swallowed hard again.

"Dear Daughter." He pronounced the words with deliberate slowness. "I am a man of few words, but this I must say."

Elena encouraged him to continue with a nod and a smile.

"The night the sailors fished you from the sea. . ." His Adam's apple bobbed up and down as he struggled to speak his mind. "I knew you were special." The quiet man spoke a little faster with each word.

"You brought light into our cabin. Into our hearts. You shared this light with us all. First my wife. . ." He encircled his wife's shoulder and drew his wife close.

"And then with my son." He smiled at Auhan and reached out to run his long fingers over the rich wood of the violin. Elena couldn't help but notice his trembling hand.

"I had lost all hope my son would ever play again." Again he had to pause as he struggled to regain control of his fragile emotions. Then, standing tall, he took a deep, rejuvenating breath and spoke with renewed strength and confidence.

"As our Auhan played those beautiful notes, I realized I had never really cherished hope in my heart." He exchanged a tender glance with his wife, and his voice softened to a whisper. "My wife, she had hope. Yet, I felt such things only through her."

He looked at Auhan, then back again to Elena. "But listening to Auhan's music. . ." His lips pursed in determination, and he nodded his head in a quick jerk. "While Auhan played, I came to understand. I can never have my own hope without this Light. I need the Light."

A glint of excitement sparked in his eyes as he spoke directly to his son. "I need the Light of my ancestors to shine within me too. The Light you have embraced, my son. As you bowed and expressed your soul with that song. . ." His face broke into a wide smile as he looked at Elena, then his son, and then stayed his gaze on his wife. "In that moment, I gave my soul over to the Christ, to the One whom Auhan's melody must glorify."

"Suleiman!" Fatima exclaimed and placed her hand upon her husband's dear face.

He looked deeply into his wife's eyes, and his joyful smile erupted into a rumble of laughter. He shook his head in amazement. He whispered, "This old, cold heart of mine could no longer ignore such a Light as Elena brought onboard."

Along with *Anne* Fatima and Auhan, Elena allowed herself to be drawn into Suleiman's strong-armed embrace, and they all celebrated this happy moment of eternal significance. As the ever quiet patriarch pounded her on the back in a most uncharacteristic display of emotion, her heart pounded in her chest with boundless bliss. She could almost hear the angels in heaven as they too rejoiced.

❧

The next morning—another beautiful day—as their little ship

drew them closer and closer to the shores of America, Auhan and Elena invited both of Auhan's parents to accompany them up onto the deck.

Although not even twenty-four hours had passed since they had declared their love for one another, it seemed like so much longer. A lifetime. To Elena, it seemed as if they had known each other forever. If Elena hadn't seen such a love blossom between Christos and her sister on the catastrophic streets of Smyrna, if she hadn't heard again and again throughout her life how quickly her parents had fallen in love, she might have been suspect. But she wasn't. Elena counted the love she and Auhan felt for one another as just another blessing from God.

"Do you have the ring?" she whispered into Auhan's ear. She referred to her mother's engagement ring, which she had taken from the handkerchief under her pillow earlier that morning. In acknowledgment, Auhan patted the pocket in his vest that protected the heirloom. Elena returned his smile. She could hardly wait to see his parents' reactions.

"*Anne, Baba,*" Auhan addressed his parents when they were all seated under the canopy, sipping tea. "Elena and I have something we'd like to tell you."

"Actually," Elena gently corrected him as she pushed a windblown strand of hair from her face, "we have something we'd like to *ask* you." Auhan gave her a quick and loving smile before turning back to his parents.

His mother looked as if her curiosity would make her jump out of her skin, whereas his father's eyes held a knowing glint. Elena suspected he knew exactly what was going on, especially when she caught him sending his son an encouraging wink. She rejoiced in the realization that Sulieman's newfound faith in the God of his ancestors had rejuvenated him. According to Auhan, the father he remembered from his childhood had now returned.

Auhan sat a little taller in his chair. "A couple of weeks ago, you offered to adopt Elena as your daughter."

Fatima nodded her head and smiled broadly. "Elena is our daughter now." She paused and qualified, "Our daughter in Christ."

Auhan's smile matched that of his mother's. "That's true but, well, as her adoptive parents, I would like to ask you both a question."

Fatima was perplexed. "You?"

"Dear." Suleiman reached out and gently squeezed his wife's hand. "Let the boy—" His thick mustache quirked as he corrected himself, "I mean, let the *man* speak."

Fatima nodded and sat back in her chair to listen and wait, albeit, impatiently.

Auhan rose and walked to the right of Elena's chair. Buddy was on her left. Placing his hand upon her shoulder, Auhan addressed his father as seriously as any young man standing before a girl's parent might.

"As Elena's adoptive father, Sir, may I request your daughter's hand in marriage?"

The words had no sooner left his mouth than *Anne* Fatima made a sound of pure glee, jumped out of her chair, and wrapped her arms around Elena.

"You will be my daughter two times—no, three times over, darling girl," she exclaimed, and both women, with smiles and nods, looked happily into each other's eyes. The miracle of a new mother for Elena wrapped around her, and Fatima's face mirrored her joy in finding a new daughter. The mother and daughter in heaven were not now, nor ever would be, forgotten. But, the gift of a new person to love helped ease the pain of missing the one who was no longer on earth.

"Well now," Suleiman drawled. "I'm not so sure, young

man," he said, causing all three to turn to him in surprise. "Just how do you propose to support my dear daughter?" Elena couldn't keep her mouth from dropping open in shock when she realized he was totally serious.

She forced her mouth closed and looked between the three of them as they silently regarded one another. Finally, she could contain herself no longer. "I haven't said much before, but my father was a very wealthy man. There will not be a need for Auhan—"

"Forgive me, Dear," Suleiman kindly cut her off, "however, I didn't ask how your father supported you. I asked how this young man was planning on doing so."

Elena looked to Auhan in dismay. In truth, they hadn't even talked about that, nor even about his profession. Money had never been an issue for Elena, and, thanks to those of her father's assets safely tucked away in banks in America, it still wouldn't be. "Really, *Baba* Suleiman," she began. But at the slight pressure of Auhan's fingers against her shoulder, she stopped.

"Your adoptive father brings forth a very good point, Elena, and one I have given thought to," he said, and her mouth again dropped open in surprise. He turned back to the older man and answered. "I will be seeking employment with an orchestra. If I am not good enough for that, then I will make, sell, and repair violins, Sir. If that is not enough, I will give music lessons to all who want to learn to love the violin as much as I do."

Suleiman stood and regarded his son for a moment. When a great big smile showed beneath his mustache—the biggest Elena had ever seen come from him—she breathed a sigh of relief. "That is acceptable work for a man who wishes to marry my daughter." He paused, and, reaching out, he took hold of Auhan's upper arms with both of his large hands and squeezed them. "And more than acceptable for my son. I'm proud of you, Auhan. Proud."

"Oh!" Fatima clapped her hands together. "A wedding to plan," she exclaimed, and they all laughed at the dreamy element in her voice. "I just love to plan celebrations! When do you plan to marry?"

Auhan looked down at Elena with a sheepish grin. "We really haven't discussed dates yet."

"Well," Elena gave her shoulders a little shrug, "I was thinking toward the end of next June."

"June?" Auhan questioned and knelt down beside her. "Beloved? That's so far away. Is it. . .because of your mourning for your father?"

She shook her head. "No, my father never agreed with that custom. He always said a Christian should not mourn for long the passing of another Christian. 'For to me to live is Christ, and to die is gain,' " she quoted from the first chapter of Philippians. "My father is in heaven with Jesus. How can I mourn that?"

"Then what is it, Beloved?" He shrugged his shoulders. "Why can we not marry sooner?"

She offered him a wistful smile. "Because," she softly answered, "I would like my sisters to be at my wedding."

"And you hope to be reunited with them by next June?"

As Elena softly nodded her head, Fatima interrupted. "Auhan, June is good," she encouraged. "You should be reunited with your brother by then too."

Auhan looked up at his mother, and Elena saw a passing shadow of pain cross over his features. "Do you really believe he will be able to make it to the Lincoln Memorial, *Anne*?"

"I do," his mother insisted.

Elena swiveled her head between the two as if she were hearing things. "What did you say?" she breathed out.

Auhan's English was heavily accented, but she was certain that she had heard him say in English, "Lincoln Memorial."

Auhan turned to her and explained. "In the event my brother, my parents, or myself were separated by this war and unable to be reunited before my parents sailed for America, we set up a rendezvous in America. My mother is a great admirer of Abraham Lincoln, so we decided to meet each May thirtieth at the memorial built in his honor in Washington—"

Elena could feel the blood drain from her face, and Auhan laid a comforting hand on her arm.

"Beloved? What is it?"

"Auhan. What is your brother's name?"

His eyes narrowed and crinkled in confusion, but he answered her. "Mehmet."

Her heart began to pound wildly.

"Mehmet!" She covered her lips with her hands in a vain attempt to contain her surprise.

Auhan fell to his knees beside her and held her hands tightly in his own. "Beloved?" he questioned with a worried frown. "Please, what is it?"

She smiled at him even as tears fell from the corners of her eyes. "Mehmet is your brother? Lincoln is your brother?" She lowered her gaze to his hands. She turned and twisted them within her own, and as she did, she finally remembered where she had seen identical ones.

"Of course, he is," she answered herself. "Your hands are exactly the same." She gave a slight laugh as her thumb traced the mole on his right thumb. "You even have a mole in the same place."

"Elena." Auhan's voice was very deep. "What you are saying is true. Mehmet and I do have identical hands. But, how do you know this?"

A look of comprehension came over *Anne* Fatima, and sh
clapped her hands in prayer as she lifted her face heaven
ward. "Oh, dear Lord, thank You. Thank You."

Elena reached out with her other hand and squeezed th
older woman's. "He lives, dear *Anne*. He lives!"

"The Turkish soldier?" Fatima questioned, and Elena vig
orously nodded her head. "Yes."

"Turkish soldier. . . ?" Even with question in his tone
Auhan voiced his dawning understanding. "The one Christo
carried?"

"Auhan." She turned back to him and swallowed to ge
control of her racing heart so that she could tell her story, he
wonderful, amazing story. "On the night my sisters and I me
Christos the second time—the night we were all fleein
Smyrna—I found out from him that the wounded man he ha
carried to our house was Turkish and," she paused, "that hi
name was Mehmet."

Auhan gasped.

"But," Elena continued, "when Christos first left him a
our house, we thought the wounded man was an America
because he was wearing an American issue serviceman'
shirt." She paused as she thought back to that time. "And th
only thing he said in his feverish state was 'Lincoln.' " Sh
gave a slight laugh. "Assuming that Lincoln was his name
my sister, father, and I called him Mr. Lincoln."

She watched as Auhan's eyes grew wide with wonder
"Mehmet. . .is truly Christos's Turkish friend? The Turk h
carried to your house?"

With her face beaming, Elena confirmed his question
"Yes. Yes, he is."

Even as joy filled his face, gravity quickly swept over it.

"But you said the man was very sick. Do you think h
survived?"

"He was very sick when Christos brought him to our house. His leg was terribly injured," she confirmed, not wanting to give false hope. "But he had a will to live, and because a friend of ours at the American consulate was able to get him aboard an American naval ship in the harbor, I think he must have made it."

She turned to Fatima and Suleiman, who were looking at her with all the ageless hope of a parent for their child. "Mehmet was alive when I last saw him on Monday, the eleventh of September. That's when he was taken aboard the American naval ship. I don't know if the doctors were able to save his leg, but I'm certain—I'm *certain* the doctors on that warship were able to make him well."

Tears streamed down Fatima's face, and Elena knew the mother's tears were happy tears, amazed tears, relieved tears, all at once.

"He must have been saying 'Lincoln,' " she whispered, "to remind himself of his rendezvous with us." She touched her hand to her chest and turned to her husband. "Suleiman, he lives! Our son lives!" she exclaimed. "The girl we fished from the sea, her family is responsible for giving our son life."

"No. It was mostly Christos," Elena corrected her. "If Christos hadn't carried him to Smyrna, Mehmet would have, without a doubt, succumbed out on the battlefield. Christos carried him on his back, literally, for days."

Suleiman shook his great head and, drawing his wife against his chest, gazed out over the vast sea surrounding their ship and said, "What an amazing God we have."

Auhan helped Elena to her feet and wrapped his arms around her. "Only God could have orchestrated this."

The two couples stood for several long moments with perfect peace and hope enfolding them. Elena broke the silence by pushing slightly back from Auhan.

"That's not all," she said. The others all turned to her with question in their eyes.

"You see, last May—" She paused and looked off into the horizon.

Was it only four months ago? The question pierced her thoughts. *It seemed like a lifetime ago.*

She swallowed hard as a somber realization struck her. *It was a lifetime ago. My father's life.* She shook her head to dispel the sad musing and turned back to them.

"My father, Sophia, and I attended the dedication to the Lincoln Memorial—"

"You attended it?" Fatima interrupted her. "That's why our rendezvous is set for May the thirtieth—the anniversary of its dedication. I so wanted to be there for the actual ceremony but—we waited—" She shrugged her thin shoulders. "In case Mehmet made it back to us."

Elena wagged her head in joyous amazement. "While we were there, we too agreed to a rendezvous at the memorial exactly a year later. I am certain I will meet my sisters and Christos on that day." She faced Auhan and turned the conversation back to his original question.

"That's the reason why, my dear love, I want to wait until June to marry."

Auhan shook his head slowly from side to side. "God had the merging of our families planned before we ever met."

Elena smiled over at him and reached into his pocket already acting as a wife might. She pulled the ring from its hiding place and held the precious stone so the rays of the morning sun caught its lines and flashed out its light.

"Dear Auhan, He had the merging of our families planned—even before the beginning of time."

"Amen," Suleiman interjected. Then her beloved Auhan

took the ring from her hand, and, bending down on one knee, he asked her, before God and his parents, to be his wife for all their earthly life.

Elena, of course, agreed.

fourteen

*May 30, 1923, Memorial Day
Lincoln Memorial
Washington, D.C.*

Everything was so different last year. Yet, so much was the
same. The secular shrine gleamed timelessly on its knoll with
the serene statue honoring Abraham Lincoln sitting within.
Elena held onto the arm of the handsome young man whom
she had grown to love during the last few months. Her feelings of affection for Auhan, which were born aboard the
Ionian Star, could not compare to the love she felt today, after
eight months of courtship. She never would have thought possible the depth of affection she now felt for Auhan.

But her thoughts turned to bittersweet memories of her
family as they approached the spot where she had stood
between Sophia and her father last year to watch the dedication ceremony of the Lincoln Memorial.

She sighed and looked up at Auhan in anxious anticipation.
"Do you think they will all come?" In truth, Elena had

expected to find Sophia and, thus, Rose and Christos through their mutual bank accounts long before this prearranged meeting. The fact that Sophia had not yet contacted the banks seemed to indicate she still hadn't arrived in America. And Elena had started to worry.

Auhan reached over and patted her right hand in its snowy white glove, which rested upon his left arm. "I believe. . ." He paused for a brief moment as though to confirm his forming words in his own heart. "I believe our God is in the miracle-making business, Elena."

His eyes looked upon her with a contagious brightness. "And this day we are going to be taking part in the miracle of a grand reunion, a reunion between loved ones and friends, something not unlike the reunion all believers will share when Jesus returns to earth."

With his words, worry erased itself from Elena's face, and a smile curved the corners of her lips. His faith amazed her. He had gone from having had none when she met him the previous September to being so full of faith, he was now a constant source of edification to her.

"You're right, of course, Auhan. They will all come today. My sisters, Christos, your brother." She spoke with faith ringing loudly in her voice. "Yes, they will all come," she reiterated with conviction. She looked back up toward the statue of the seated President Lincoln and the pavilion built to house it, which had been fashioned after the Parthenon of Athens. In the gleaming light of the Lincoln Memorial's white marble there existed the complete antithesis to that which had run rampant across the city of Smyrna during those black days the previous September.

In the light of the early morning sun, the monument gleamed pristine and new. But the sight of it brought her thoughts back to similar Greek edifices to be found throughout the Hellenic world of the Mediterranean. She glanced back at the Washington Monument, which shot up into the sky. Further on, the United States Capitol building gleamed in the light of the rising sun. It was all so beautiful. Beautiful and new. She sighed.

Auhan leaned toward her and asked with softness lacing his words, "What are you thinking?"

Elena slightly shook her head. "So many things, but mostly I hope America—this land founded and built by people who believed Christ is God's Son—is never taken over by a people who don't believe in Him, as we saw happen in Asia Minor. This is my greatest hope for this country, this beloved land."

"Mine too, my dear," Auhan nodded his head. From the moment he had set foot upon America's green and golden shores, he had fallen in love with this land. It was his home now. And one he never planned to leave. He leaned over and planted a kiss upon Elena's forehead. He had started doing so when she had fretted that her scars had left her looking ugly. Auhan had taken to kissing them as a way of assuring her that, although they did exist, they were not displeasing, at least not to him. It was a habit now, but one he never took for granted. Those scars, only partially hidden by her hair, were a poignant reminder of what evil had cost her, cost them all.

So many lives had been lost, and many more were still being uprooted by it. Earlier in the year, the Treaty of Lausanne had implemented a "population exchange." This exchange enforced the relocation of almost one and a half million Greeks, whose families had built some of Asia Minor's most glorious cities during the previous three thousand years, in addition to the displacement of well over three hundred thousand Turks who had settled in Greece. Auhan shook his head. So much pain. How could governments justify forcing people—any people—from their home?

But Auhan wasn't naïve. Although he never talked about it to anyone, he remembered the mass grave.

He knew that the population exchange was actually the only way the governments of the allied powers, after their poor decision-making during and after the Great War, could save the remaining Christians of Asia Minor. If the Christians weren't forced out by international politics, they would, at the hands of the Turkish government, suffer the same fate met by millions of martyred Christians—Armenians, Greeks and others—over the previous thirty years. And more little babies would have to suffer like the baby in the blue sweater who still came to haunt Auhan.

Auhan slightly shook his head and sent a prayer heavenward, asking God to take away the tormenting image of the child.

As always, God did.

Where it used to stay within his head for days at a time, it now only came to torment him at odd moments. Auhan suspected it always would. But with the Lord Jesus Christ in his life, the vision no longer debilitated him.

He looked over at his parents. They stood directly in front of the Lincoln Memorial, just below the first step leading up toward the statue. In excited expectation, they were casting their eyes about for Mehmet. Auhan was so grateful to God they had left their home while they could. They would have been caught right in the middle of the population exchange and would never have made it to America otherwise.

Auhan looked back at the Capitol in the distance. Elena was right. He hoped Christianity was never forced from this land as it had been from Asia Minor and so many other areas of the world. He hoped people never forgot the liberty brought to people through their belief in the truth of Jesus Christ.

Reaching into his pocket, he took out an American silver dollar and turned to the side with the eagle. He looked at the inscription engraved between its wings. "In God We Trust," Auhan silently read America's motto and sighed. He just hoped the people of America never forgot that the God referred to on their money was God as revealed by Jesus Christ.

Elena tensed by his side, bringing his attention back to her. "What is it?"

"There," she breathed out and pointed in the direction of the Washington Monument. The silhouettes of three people—a very tall man, a woman, and a young girl—could be seen walking toward them. "It has to be them. No one is as tall as Christos." She qualified what made the three, just visible near the far end of the recently completed Reflecting Pool, different from the other elegantly clad people strolling in the morning sunshine.

Auhan chuckled. "This is America, Elena. Many tall men grow here." He wanted to keep things light, just in case the three were not her Sophia, Rose, and Christos. He didn't want her to get excited, only to be bitterly disappointed.

"We will wait until they get a little closer." She paused and squinted against the sun. "Oh, I wish the sun had decided to rise in the west today. I can't see anything with the glare."

Auhan chuckled, glad to hear her joke. As long as she could make light of the situation, she would be fine—even if the people coming toward them were not three of the four for whom they anxiously awaited this day.

When the threesome were closer to the Lincoln Memorial than they were to the Washington Monument, Elena started walking toward them, pulling Auhan along with her. Buddy, as always, was right at her heals. "Come on," she said. "We'll just stroll casually in that direction until—"

"El—e—na!" a woman's voice called out, and Elena held out her hand for Auhan to stop.

"Sophia?" Elena squeaked out the name, her volume barely louder than a whisper.

"El—e—na," the woman called out again.

Elena responded with a half-laugh, half-sob. "So—ph—ia!"

"Elena?!" came the return, this time in a chorus of three voices—that of a man, a woman, and a child.

"It's them, Auhan! It's them." She waved her arms in a wide, swooping arc and began to shout as she took off in a run toward the trio. "It's me! It's me!"

Laughing and sobbing, Elena covered the distance between herself and her sister as if wings were on her feet. Within seconds their arms were around one another, and they were kissing each other—laughing and crying all at the same time.

"Sophia! Rose!" Elena swept both her tall, elegant sister and the beautiful little girl into her arms. "Oh, we've found one another! We've found one another!" As she reached for Christos, she wished she had another pair of arms with which to hold her dear ones.

She felt herself being lifted off the ground in a mighty embrace. "Christos," she squealed in happy surprise.

"Give your brother-in-law a hug, little Elena," he boomed out with a voice that matched his body. Not the least surprised by his news, Elena hugged him closer.

"I knew you were going to be my brother one day. I just knew it," she bubbled. When Christos put her down, she reached for her sisters again. "Dear Sophia. I'm so happy for you. Knowing you had Christos and Rose kept me from worrying about you."

Sophia wiped the corners of her eyes with her crochet-bordered handkerchief. "And, Dear Sister, it was their faith that edified me enough to function without knowing for sure if you would be here today."

"God never took His eyes off of me," Elena assured her sister as she allowed her to scrutinize the telling burns on her face. She hastily relayed the fantastic story of her rescue at sea, taking care to credit the special family that had nursed her back to health.

Feeling a tug on her skirt, Elena reached down and scooped a giggling Rose into her arms. "Little sister, I'm so glad to see you."

"Me too, but—" Rose paused and rolled her shining eyes. "I don't think you should call me your little sister."

"Why not? Don't you want to be my little sister any longer?" Elena searched the girl's grinning face for a clue as to why she would say such a thing.

"Yes, but," Christos interrupted, and with a wide smile cutting across his face, he took Rose from Elena with one arm while his other went comfortably around Sophia's shoulders, "what Rose probably means is that you are now her aunt, not her sister."

Elena's mouth dropped open as she stared at first Christos, then Sophia.

"After we married, we legally adopted Rose as our daughter," Sophia explained.

Elena thought her happy heart could not contain any more good news. Bringing her face right up next to Rose's, she said, "So now you have a father, a mother, and an aunt."

Rose nodded her head vigorously. "But that's not all," she exclaimed and looked over at her new mother as if she might burst.

Understanding the look, Elena exclaimed, "You have a secret!"

A grin spread Rose's pixie face, and she bobbed her head up and down so hard, her curls bounced around her shoulders like puppets on a string. Sophia laughed in her delightful, refined way. It was a sound from their past that thrilled Elena all the way down to her toes, even as she regarded her sister in happy question.

"Come now, tell me," Elena insisted with her eyes wide and bright.

"Well," Sophia looked shyly but lovingly up at Christos. "Rose will have a sister or a brother soon too."

Elena's eyes widened even more as she noticed, for the first time, her sister's expanding figure. "A baby!" she whispered and hugged Sophia close to her again. "I'm so happy for you—" Her look included the three of them. "For all of you."

Elena reached for Auhan's hand. "We have news too. This very wonderful man, Auhan, is soon to be my husband."

"What? When?" Sophia's surprise registered in her monosyllabic questions.

"As soon as we can get your dresses made," Elena said. "We waited so that you could be at our wedding."

"Oh, Elena, Auhan. Your news gladdens my heart." Sophia threw her arms around both Elena and her husband-to-be in a congratulatory hug. And, even though Elena knew her sister was more than a little curious to know all about this handsome, young man with the Turkish name, she also knew Sophia trusted her to choose the right mate.

"We so wanted to wait for you to be at our wedding," Sophia explained to Elena, "but Christos and Rose didn't have the necessary immigration documents for entry into America, and such things take many, many months, years, to receive—if ever. We were advised that our marriage and Rose's subsequent adoption would be the most expedient way for them to obtain the proper permissions."

Elena watched as Sophia looked into her husband's eyes.

She gave him a dimpled smile and breathed a deep sigh of contentment. "Since Christos and I knew from the time we met in Smyrna that God intended us for one another. . .Well, we saw this as the answer—"

"You obviously made the right decision," Elena interrupted. She remembered back to how Sophia's thoughts of Christos had kept her sister going after their father had died.

Sophia gave Elena a smile and a gentle nod before she continued. "We decided on a quiet but lovely ceremony at a sixth-century chapel in Athens. Then, as husband and wife, we were able to legally adopt Rose as our daughter." Elena gave in to her urge to tousle little Rose's hair as her sister spoke.

"Only two things survived from all the treasures I had sewn into my clothing before we fled Smyrna. My papers verifying my American citizenship and one of Mother's necklaces. We were able to sell the necklace, and we lived off the proceeds of the sale." She continued after a brief pause. "But God knew what He was doing. If I hadn't had those things, we wouldn't have made it here today."

Christos shook his lowered head from side to side. "Greece has opened her doors to all the refugees fleeing Asia Minor and the population of the country is increasing at an astronomical rate. But, there is much misery. After these many years of war, Greece is so poor."

"It still took months for us to accomplish all the necessary requirements for our passage here," Sophia said. "Our ship arrived in New York only yesterday, and we traveled directly from there to here." She motioned down to their clothes, and Elena noticed they were still wearing traveling outfits.

"So, that's why you haven't gone to the banks," Elena commented. "I left messages for you, telling you where I was living. I must admit, I was getting concerned when I heard nothing from you." She looked over at Auhan. "I don't know what I would have done if I hadn't had my man of faith to strengthen and support me."

Sophia extended her hand to Auhan in a show of gratitude. Then, she turned again to Elena.

"You do understand, don't you, why I couldn't wait for you to be at our wedding? I know we had planned for—"

Elena signaled for her sister to stop. "Dear Sophia. I don't mind. Not at all." She laughed gaily. "The only things to have survived my journey were our mother's cross, her engagement ring, and. . ." Elena paused long enough for suspense to fill the air. "Her wedding ring."

"Her wedding ring!"

The wedding ring had always been intended for Sophia, the engagement ring for her. She knew how much it meant to Sophia to have something of their mother's.

"It's sitting safely in my jewelry case, waiting for you in the home I bought for us all near the Capitol." Elena sent Christos a quick smile.

"Actually, the ring is waiting not for you, but for Christos." A look of bewilderment colored her sister's face, so Elena hastened to finish her sentence. "For Christos will be the one to place it on your finger." Sophia's expression portrayed her utter happiness as Elena shifted to a more serious note.

"But dear Sophia, more than anything, I'm so thankful that you weren't left orphaned and alone." Her look included Rose and Christos. "I'm thankful you joined together to make a family. I might not yet be married to Auhan, but in his parents, I have had the love of a mother and a father." She pointed to the older couple, who stood by the marble stairs of the memorial. "They are the very special people who took me into their cabin and into their hearts after my ordeal in the sea. They are the ones who nursed me back to health. Come, let me introduce you."

Amid much talking and laughing, the happy band walked over to Fatima and Suleiman. Rose and Buddy frolicked around the adults with the youthful abandon that every dog and child should have. The two were becoming fast friends.

Fatima held out her hands to Elena as they approached. "Your sisters?" she asked. At Elena's nod, Fatima opened her arms to Sophia and Rose. "Oh, I'm so glad. So thankful you are reunited."

"Thank you, dear people, for caring for my sister." Sophia's gaze included them both.

Suleiman smiled beneath his mustache. "Ah, My Dear. I think your sister cared for us every bit as much as we cared for her."

Sophia laughed and looked at her sister with a knowing glint. "She has a way of doing that."

From out of the corner of her eye, Elena noticed Auhan shaking hands with Christos, and she seized upon the lull in her circle of conversation to eavesdrop on the pair's dialogue.

"Excuse me, Sir, but have we met before?" Christos squinted, and his brow furrowed in deep curiosity as he studied Auhan. "You seem so familiar, and I'm never one to forget a face."

"No, Christos, we haven't met," Auhan rasped. "But you have met my brother."

Elena knew her beloved well enough to know that he was fighting to maintain control of his emotions. Over the past months, Auhan had often spoken of the day when he would meet Christos and get to thank him face-to-face for carrying his brother across the battlefields to safety. If Mehmet managed to keep the rendezvous with his family today, it would be due to the aid and compassionate spirit of this gentle giant, Christos.

"Look carefully, Christos," Elena instructed, and Christos's brows knit together as he obviously searched his brain to try and place the familiar stranger. "Think. Who does he remind you of?"

Elena tilted her head to her sister. "Sophia? How about you? Do you notice anything familiar about Auhan?"

Sophia looked at Auhan carefully. "He does remind me of someone," she shook her head. "But I can't—"

"Look at his hands, Sophia," Elena prompted.

Auhan lifted his hands for all to see while Suleiman and Fatima smiled at each other. Sophia reached out to Auhan and held his hands with her gloved fingers. "They seem so familiar—"

"Mehmet," Christos whispered, for once without a loud voice. He looked from Auhan's hands to his face. "You're Mehmet's brother?"

Auhan nodded.

Christos turned to the older couple. "And you. . .are Mehmet's parents?"

"Lincoln?" Sophia breathed out the name by which she still thought of Mehmet—the young man she had diligently nursed over a period of several days the previous September in Smyrna. At everyone's affirmative nods, Christos and Sophia exchanged looks of total amazement before they turned back to the others.

"But, how did you," Christos motioned between Auhan and Elena. "I mean. Mehmet? He lives?"

"Yes, my friend," a man's soft voice answered from behind the happy group. "He lives."

And, as a single body, Elena and the precious members of her family all turned in the direction of the one speaking. She could hardly believe her ears. Or her eyes.

There stood Mehmet! He leaned on a cane, but he was standing—and on two legs, not one.

Joy and laughter and everything good filled the air surrounding the happy, complete reunion of family and friends. Their voices tumbled together in melodious cacophony as they became acquainted or reacquainted with one another. Elena rejoiced along with *Anne* Fatima, *Baba* Suleiman, and Auhan to hear that Mehmet too had learned to trust the God of his distant ancestors.

And they all marveled at how God had woven the fabric of their lives together so miraculously.

For Elena and her beloved family, Memorial Day of 1923 was the first of many such days of reunion and remembrance—one which they were to keep each and every anniversary of the Lincoln Memorial dedication. For the rest of their lives. Their very long lives.

A Letter To Our Readers

Dear Reader:

In order that we might better contribute to your reading enjoyment, we would appreciate your taking a few minutes to respond to the following questions. We welcome your comments and read each form and letter we receive. When completed, please return to the following:

Rebecca Germany, Fiction Editor
Heartsong Presents
PO Box 719
Uhrichsville, Ohio 44683

1. Did you enjoy reading *Remnant of Light* by Taylor James?
   ☐ Very much! I would like to see more books
      by this author!
   ☐ Moderately. I would have enjoyed it more if

   _____

   _____

   _____

2. Are you a member of **Heartsong Presents**? Yes ☐ No ☐
   If no, where did you purchase this book?_____

   _____

3. How would you rate, on a scale from 1 (poor) to 5 (superior), the cover design?_____

4. On a scale from 1 (poor) to 10 (superior), please rate the following elements.

   _____ Heroine   _____ Plot

   _____ Hero   _____ Inspirational theme

   _____ Setting   _____ Secondary characters

5. These characters were special because_____
_____
_____

6. How has this book inspired your life?_____
_____
_____

7. What settings would you like to see covered in future
   Heartsong Presents books?_____
_____
_____

8. What are some inspirational themes you would like to see
   treated in future books?_____
_____
_____

9. Would you be interested in reading other **Heartsong
   Presents** titles?   Yes ❑   No ❑

10. Please check your age range:
    ❑ Under 18   ❑ 18-24   ❑ 25-34
    ❑ 35-45   ❑ 46-55   ❑ Over 55

Name _____
Occupation _____
Address _____
City _____ State _____ Zip _____
Email _____

Hearts♥ng Presents
Love Stories Are Rated G!

That's for godly, gratifying, and of course, great! If you love a thrilling love story but don't appreciate the sordidness of some popular paperback romances, **Heartsong Presents** is for you. In fact, **Heartsong Presents** is the *only inspirational romance book club* featuring love stories where Christian faith is the primary ingredient in a marriage relationship.

Sign up today to receive your first set of four never-before-published Christian romances. Send no money now; you will receive a bill with the first shipment. You may cancel at any time without obligation, and if you aren't completely satisfied with any selection, you may return the books for an immediate refund!

Imagine. . .four new romances every four weeks—two historical, two contemporary—with men and women like you who long to meet the one God has chosen as the love of their lives. . .all for the low price of $9.97 postpaid.

To join, simply complete the coupon below and mail to the address provided. **Heartsong Presents** romances are rated G for another reason: They'll arrive *Godspeed!*